# MAFIA KINGS: DARIO

A DARK MAFIA ROMANCE SERIES

BOOK ONE

OLIVIA THORN

WWW.OLIVIATHORN.COM

# ALSO BY OLIVIA THORN

Mafia Kings: Dario

Mafia Kings: Adriano

Mafia Kings: Massimo

Mafia Kings: Lars (coming soon)

\*\*\*

**AS OLIVIA THORNE**

**Billionaire Romance**

All That He Wants (Volume 1)

All That He Loves (Volume 2)

The Billionaire's Wedding (Volume 3)

\*\*\*

The Billionaire's Kiss (Parts 1-4)

The Billionaire's Obsession (Part 5)

\*\*\*

**Motorcycle Romance**

Midnight Desire (Part 1)

Midnight Lust (Part 2)

Midnight Deceit (Part 3)

Midnight Obsession (Part 4)

\*\*\*

**Rockstar Romance**

(Careful - cheating in Part 3, Why Choose, HFN ending)

Rock Me Hard (Part 1)

Rock All Night (Part 2)

Hard As Rock (Part 3)

# 1

Alessandra

I lived a quiet and boring life working in my father's tiny café in Tuscany...

Until the night *he* walked in.

*Il Mostro.*

'The monster.'

The devilishly handsome mafia don Dario Rosolini.

He and his brothers run this region of Italy... and they take everything they want.

Apparently *il Mostro* thought that applied to me, as well.

From the beginning, he made clear to his brothers that I was his, and ONLY his.

But I was sheltered before I met him – a good Catholic girl.

Now I faced the devil himself.

The only thing protecting me was a promise he made to my father...

The same night he spirited me away to his dark fairytale estate.

No matter how many temptations he put in my path, though, I swore never to give in.

Not just because I'm afraid of him (although I am)...

But because, deep down, I grew to desire him...

To *want* him more than anything I had ever wanted in my entire life...

With a fire that threatened to consume me like the flames of hell.

But I know what he is.

A *mafioso.*

A murderer.

He is *il Mostro*... the beast... the devil himself.

And no matter how much I might want him...

Giving in to him will ruin me forever.

# 2

I lived near a town called Mensano, about an hour south of Firenze – which you probably know as Florence.

Mensano is a tiny but beautiful place. It was a walled village from medieval times that looked out over the gorgeous fields of Tuscany. Perhaps 200 people live inside the town walls.

But I didn't even live *in* Mensano. I lived along the mountain road to the village.

My father owned a café visited by locals and a few tourists passing through on their way to somewhere else.

My mother died when I was only 12 years old, and ever since then I was his only helper in the café. He would cook the few dishes we offered on the menu, and I would serve the customers.

It was a lonely, boring life.

I loved my father, but it was *not* what I wanted for myself.

I was 20 years old. I had hoped to move out when I finished school at 18 – perhaps to Florence! – but I didn't have nearly enough money.

And my father had begged me to stay. Without my help, the café would go under because he couldn't afford to pay anyone else.

Plus he said he would die of loneliness without me, which broke my heart.

So I stayed.

Yet I yearned for something – *anything* – else.

I soon learned to be careful what you wish for.

I lived with Papa above the café. Our closest neighbor was a 65-year-old widow who would walk a quarter of a mile every morning to have coffee and flirt with my father.

At 51, Papa was much younger than her. He had been older than my mother, and they had had me much later in life (at least compared with what was common in rural Italy).

Despite six years of flirting, the widow still hadn't made any headway.

Papa had loved my mother fiercely, and he still mourned her passing every day.

Sometimes I felt like my own life had ended with hers.

Seven days a week, I took orders for coffee, pastries, and the occasional meal.

On Sundays I would walk to the church in Mensano for mass because we were too poor to own a car. Then I had to walk back home in time for afternoon lunch in the café.

My father was *not* devout. He never attended mass, and despite my complaints, he forced me to work on the Sabbath.

Every Sunday I would joke, "If I have to spend an extra year in Purgatory because of you – "

"Didn't you hear, Alessandra? The Pope got rid of Purgatory years ago," he would tease me. "And you don't do anything bad enough to go to hell, so you're fine."

"That's because there's nothing to *do* around here that's bad enough for hell."

Little did I know, something 'bad enough' would come and find *me*.

It was a Monday night. I remember the day because it was odd to have *anyone* in the café for dinner on a Monday, much less a stranger.

He was in his 30s and ugly, like a toad with fat lips. I could tell by his accent that he was from the north, far away from Florence. When he came in, he demanded a table where he could sit with his back against the wall.

He was curt and rude and had a nasty habit of staring at my breasts whenever he talked to me. I dress very conservatively, so it wasn't like I was inviting his gaze – but he still looked at me like a piece of meat, which made my skin crawl.

As soon as I took his order, I retreated to the far end of the café and waited for my father to finish cooking his meal.

The ugly man was constantly darting his eyes around the stone walls of the café. No one else was in there except for him, me, and Papa working in the kitchen – but the man seemed afraid that a boogeyman would suddenly appear from the shadows.

Apparently he knew something I didn't.

I had just delivered his *pollo al limone* – chicken with lemon – when the ugly man said something odd in his northern-accented Italian: "Tell your father my compliments to the chef."

I was struck by the fact that he said it before he'd even had a bite of the food.

Then I realized I hadn't told him my father was the cook.

There was no way the ugly man could have *known* my father had cooked his meal unless he had been here before... or somehow knew about the café.

I thought of asking him how he knew, but I disliked him so much that I just nodded and went back to my perch at the far end of the café.

After ogling me some more, the ugly man began wolfing down his food.

Then the door to the café opened up and another man walked in.

He was tall, well over six feet. He was dressed in a black trench coat and wore a black hat, so it was hard to see his features – but his short blond beard and icy blue eyes suggested he wasn't Italian. He was, however, *very* handsome.

Just as I was about to welcome him, the stranger turned to the ugly man and pulled out a pistol.

The ugly man froze with a forkful of food in his mouth. Then he scrambled for something in his pocket – probably a gun, too – but he wasn't fast enough.

*BANG BANG BANG!*

Fire exploded from the blond stranger's gun.

The ugly man's body jerked three times. Then he slumped to the side and fell out of his chair.

I screamed in horror as blood pooled on the stone floor.

The blond man turned to me, and I felt an electric spark as his icy blue eyes met mine.

I was sure I was dead – that his gun would point at *me* next –

But instead the handsome stranger put his weapon away and hurried out of the café.

My father ran into the room just as the front door banged shut.

My father cried out, "Alessandra, what happened?!"

I just stared at the corpse in shock.

The only dead body I had ever seen was at my mother's funeral...

And I had certainly never seen a man murdered before my eyes.

Before too long, I would see many, many more.

My father took one look at the dead man and suddenly became even more frightened.

Later, I would wonder if he recognized the ugly man – though in my shock, I didn't consider the possibility at the time.

"Did you see who did this?" he whispered.

I nodded mutely.

He grabbed my shoulders and forced me to look at him.

"You must *never* tell anyone what he looked like," he said hoarsely. "Especially not the police."

"But – "

"PROMISE me."

I promised him.

It was probably the one thing that saved both our lives.

# 3

The local police arrived almost immediately – but as soon as they heard what had happened, they called Florence. No one else was qualified to investigate such a brazen assassination.

The detective who showed up two hours later, though, seemed bored. Perhaps he felt that a killing in the middle of nowhere was beneath him.

He asked me what had happened. I told him everything, but said that I had only seen a man in a black trench coat and hat – that I hadn't seen his face.

After I finished speaking, Papa gave me an encouraging smile.

I felt guilty for lying, but I persuaded myself that it was more important to obey my father.

The detective searched the ugly man's clothes and found a pistol in his jacket pocket.

So he *had* been scrambling for a gun when the blond stranger had shot him...

The detective ordered the local ambulance to take the body away. Then he had the man's car towed back to Florence.

It was nearly 11 o'clock at night when they all departed... and I was left with the horrible task of cleaning up the blood on the stone floor.

"I'll help you," my father said quietly, and went to the kitchen to get buckets and brushes.

While he was gone, I heard the door open behind me.

I thought it was one of the police returning, so I wasn't afraid.

But I *became* afraid as soon I turned around.

Three men stood by the doorway.

All three were relatively young – in their mid- to late 20s.

All three wore expensive dress suits, and all three were incredibly handsome in their own way.

Their features were close enough that they seemed to be related –

That was where the similarities ended.

To the left was a mountain of a man – at least 200 centimeters, or 6'6" for you Americans. He had massively broad shoulders and enormous muscles beneath his dark suit. He reminded me of a circus strongman from old black-and-white movies. He had a full head of brown hair and a neatly trimmed beard. I thought of him as an *orso* – a bear. Despite his imposing size, his warm brown eyes were kind.

To the right was a shorter man, though he still stood at least 6'2". His hair was dark brown and slightly curled, his face had just a bit of scruff, and he wore a flashy blue suit with a silk shirt. He was trim and muscular.

Though not nearly as big as the Bear, he was more threatening. His handsome face was furious, as though someone had insulted him, and he scowled like he wanted to kill me.

I immediately thought of him as the Hothead.

But he was not the most frightening... *or the most handsome.*

That was the man in the center.

He was in the middle as far as height – about 6'4" – but his shoulders were almost as broad as the Bear's.

His jet-black hair was swept back from his face, and he wore a short black beard trimmed to perfection.

His cheekbones were like a fashion model's. Piercing black eyes stared out from under his furrowed brow.

He wore a navy blue suit with a light blue shirt open at the throat. I could see tattoos at the top of his chest, extending up his neck.

He appeared to be the oldest of the group, possibly close to 30.

The thing that stood out about him – other than his devastatingly good looks – was the sense of authority that emanated from him. The other two men seemed to be his subordinates.

The Bear looked threatening because of his size...

And the Hothead looked unsafe because of his anger...

But the man in the middle was mysterious and calm... and that made him all the more dangerous.

Not to mention that he stared at me like a hawk looking at a baby rabbit.

I stared back at him, my mouth slightly agape.

Then he smiled the tiniest bit... just a slight upturning of the corner of his mouth...

And my heart skipped a beat.

"I understand something happened here tonight," he said in a deep, smoky voice.

I swallowed hard and nodded, unable to speak.

I felt like I was drowning in his eyes – and then his voice mesmerized me even further.

Just at that moment, my father emerged from the kitchen. "Excuse me, we're clo– "

But the words died in his throat when he saw the three men.

Actually, when he saw the man in the middle.

The handsome stranger looked at him. "Do you know who I am?"

"O-of course, Don Rosolini."

As soon as Papa said the name, my blood froze in my veins.

*Don Rosolini.*

*Il Mostro.*

The Monster.

The Rosolinis were a family of *mafiosos,* and they had controlled this region of Tuscany for over 50 years. The grandfather had come from Sicily half a century before and staked out his claim with blood and fire.

The name inspired fear. No one crossed the Rosolinis – *no one.*

Those who did either lived to regret it... or disappeared without a trace.

The head of the family was often referred to as *il Mostro* for his horrendous acts of violence against his enemies. The don did not hurt innocent local folk, who fell under his protection – but he destroyed other *mafiosos* who dared infringe on his territory.

But the name *il Mostro* was always whispered, as though speaking it might summon the devil himself.

Certainly my father appeared terrified. He trembled slightly as he said, "I was so sorry to hear about your father, God rest his soul."

*...your father?*

*God rest his soul?*

This was news to me.

"*Grazie,*" the mystery man said. "What's your name?"

"Enzo Calvano. May I offer you a drink, Don Rosolini?"

"The only thing I need is information. I understand that a man was killed in your establishment earlier tonight."

"Yes," my father said as he gestured at the curdled pool of blood on the stones.

"Did you see the killer?"

"No," my father said. "I was in the kitchen."

Don Rosolini turned his dark eyes to me. "Did your... daughter see him? I assume she is your daughter?"

"Yes," both my father and I said at once.

The *mafioso* smiled as he stared into my soul. "Did you see the killer?"

Before I could answer, my father hastily interrupted. "No, she only saw a man in a black jacket and hat."

The Hothead spoke for the first time. "He asked HER, old man, not y– "

Don Rosolini held up one hand, and the Hothead immediately stopped talking.

The mystery man turned to me. "Well? Did you see him or not?"

I glanced at my father –

"Don't look at him. Look at me," the *mafioso* ordered.

I gazed into his eyes, which seemed to pull me into their depths.

"And I warn you," he continued, "you should *always* tell me the truth. Because you have no idea what I know... and if I catch you in a lie, the consequences will be *very* unpleasant. Do you understand?"

I swallowed hard. "Yes."

"Did you see the killer?"

"...y-yes."

"What did he look like?"

"He was tall... blond, with a beard... blue eyes. He might have been Swedish."

I glanced over at my father, who looked absolutely terrified. I wondered if I had done the right thing.

When the don spoke again, his voice was quiet. "Why did you lie to the police?"

I frowned in astonishment. "How did you know that?"

He smiled, and it sent shivers down my spine. "I have friends in the *Questura.*"

The *Questura* was the police department based out of Florence.

So the devil had infiltrated law enforcement, as well.

"It was my fault, *signore*," my father said in a pleading voice. "She is my only child, and I did not want her to get wrapped up in this... this – "

"Situation?" Don Rosolini finished for him.

"...yes."

The mystery man regarded my father for a long moment before he spoke. "Understandable. She is, I am sure, your most treasured possession."

"I am no one's *possession*," I snapped –

Which caused quite a response.

My father looked like he might have a heart attack.

The Bear looked surprised.

The Hothead got even angrier.

But the mafia don regarded me with amusement.

"Of course not," he said in that deep, smoky voice. "I only meant that your father treasures you... and should not lie to me again in a wasted effort to ensure your safety. Would you not agree, *signore?*"

"Y-yes, *padrone,*" my father stuttered.

"Good. What was the victim doing in your café?"

My father gave a forced laugh that was full of fear. "Why, the same as anyone else, I suppose! Just having a meal."

"Your café is rather off the beaten path. He didn't come in for another reason?"

"No! I mean... not that I know of."

Suddenly I thought of the ugly man's strange words:

*Tell your father my compliments to the chef.*

I also thought about how I had suspected the ugly man knew my father –

But I was afraid to voice those suspicions.

I was also afraid of lying to the *mafioso* again –

But he hadn't asked me anything.

So I wouldn't technically be lying if I held my tongue... which I did.

The stranger looked at my father like he was trying to see deep into his soul. With those piercing eyes of his, I almost believed he could.

"Let me take him out back," the Hothead snapped. *"I'll* loosen his tongue."

The don raised one hand, and the Hothead went back to seething in silence.

But the handsome stranger never looked away from my father.

Finally he said, "The man who visited your establishment tonight... the one who died over there..."

He gestured to the curdled pool of blood.

"...I received word that he was part of a plot against me and my family. But I don't know what the plot entailed."

"That's horrible," my father said earnestly.

"Indeed. If you hear anything of interest, you should contact me immediately. Massimo, give the man our number."

The Bear reached into his suit and produced a business card. It looked ludicrously small between his giant fingers.

So the Bear's name was Massimo...

My father took the card and nodded. "Of course, *padrone*."

"I would greatly appreciate your cooperation in this matter."

"Absolutely, Don Rosolini."

"And until I am sure I have your utmost cooperation... I'm going to take your daughter with me as collateral."

The words stunned me – and they equally surprised my father.

Papa blinked. "Um... excuse me, *padrone?*"

"Are you deaf?" the Hothead snarled.

The *mafioso* glared at the Hothead. "Adriano."

So the Hothead's name was Adriano.

After the one-word rebuke, Adriano fell silent.

Then Don Rosolini turned back to my father. "I repeat: I'm taking your daughter as collateral while you gather more information for me."

"What?!" I cried out angrily. "No!"

All four men – the *mafioso*, Massimo, Adriano, and my father – looked at me in surprise.

Of course, my father's surprise was more like horrified shock.

The mafia don's expression was far more amused.

"I am afraid you don't have a choice in the matter," he informed me.

"Is that *so?*" I snapped.

I turned to walk out of the room –

But Massimo the Bear stepped in front of me. His speed was surprising for a man of his size.

He looked down at me and gently shook his head like, *That wouldn't be a good idea.*

I stepped back and didn't move.

"*Padrone...* please, I beg of you, not my daughter," my father whispered.

"Don't worry – she'll be well taken care of. You may have her back when you have more information about your visitor this evening."

"But sir, I know nothing – "

"Which is why I know you'll find out *something* for me." The don turned to Massimo. "Take her to get her belongings."

"Sir – " my father said as he stepped forward abruptly, which I guess was slightly threatening –

Because Adriano shot forward, grabbed my father by the collar, and pushed him back.

"NO!" I screamed.

The head *mafioso* tilted his head to the side, and Adriano relaxed his hold.

"Don Rosolini..." my father whispered, "Alessandra is a good girl... she goes to mass every Sunday... she's a virgin, *padrone...*"

My face flushed scarlet.

I *was* a virgin, it was true – because of my religious beliefs.

...but also partially due to a lack of opportunity in the small village where I lived.

To hear my father say it out loud was mortifying.

The handsome *mafioso* fixed me with a stare like he was about to tear off my dress. "Interesting information, to be sure – but what does it have to do with me?"

"Sir, your reputation precedes you," my father whispered. "You are a worldly man... and you reap where you do not sow. My daughter is an innocent..."

The *mafioso* spoke to my father, but he walked slowly towards *me.* "Are you suggesting that I might take advantage of your daughter?"

I felt fear at his words – but my face blazed even hotter.

The horror of this stranger and my father discussing me this way – it was too much to bear.

And yet, as I looked into the stranger's mesmerizing eyes, I felt a different kind of heat bloom between my legs.

"I..." my father said, then stopped. He was obviously afraid of offending *il Mostro.*

"I give you my word," the *mafioso* said as he stopped just inches away from me. "I will not take your daughter's virginity..."

The smile he gave me was both seductive and terribly cruel.

"...until she begs me to do so."

My father didn't know what to say to that. He was stunned into silence.

I, on the other hand, was not.

"I am not a *whore* to be bargained over," I snarled.

With lightning speed, the *mafioso* pressed against my body and grasped the hair at the back of my neck.

He pulled my head back with a gentle tug so I was staring up at him.

I could feel him against me – his muscles beneath his suit as they pressed against my soft body.

I was terrified –

And yet at the same time, lust seemed to engulf me like fire.

Other than my father, I had never been this close to a man before in my life –

And certainly not the most attractive and powerful man I had ever seen.

My heart hammered in my chest from both fear and excitement.

He was pressed so firmly against me that I was sure he could feel my heartbeat.

Then he leaned down to whisper in my ear.

I caught a whiff of his cologne – subtle, expensive, and overwhelmingly masculine.

His lips brushed my ear, and my eyes half-closed in a haze of desire.

"You *will* be my whore," he whispered. "But *only* for me... and no one else."

Then he let go of my hair and pulled away from me.

I was furious –

I was afraid –

And yet there were stirrings inside me more powerful than anything I'd ever felt before.

"Massimo, take her to get her things while I talk to her father," the stranger said.

Massimo gestured with his head like, *Come on.*

I looked at my father.

He glanced at Don Rosolini... then looked back at me and nodded.

I angrily went to my room upstairs with the Bear trailing along behind me.

# 4

Massimo stood guard as I retrieved several dresses and a negligee from my wardrobe.

When it came time to get my bras and underwear, I cleared my throat. "Could you...?"

"Oh," he said in a voice even deeper than his boss's. Then he looked away, almost in embarrassment. "Of course."

I gathered the things from my dresser and wrapped them inside my dresses. "Alright."

He looked at my bundle of clothes and frowned. "Don't you have a suitcase?"

"No."

He looked mystified.

I shrugged. "I've never gone anywhere before, so there was never a need."

He raised his eyebrows and tilted his head like, *Makes sense.*

Then he started to lead the way back down to the café...

But I stood still, afraid of what would happen when I went back downstairs.

Massimo realized I wasn't following and looked back.

Rather than becoming impatient, he smiled gently. "Nothing will happen to you. When my brother gives his word, he never breaks it."

I looked at him in shock. "He's your brother?!"

"So is Adriano. There are six of us."

I realized it should not have surprised me so much. The *Cosa Nostra* was all about fathers, sons, brothers, uncles, cousins...

There was no reason they would not all be involved in the family business.

The family business being crime... and murder.

I shook my head. "I'm not worried about *me* so much as I am about what will happen to my father."

"If he wasn't involved in whatever conspiracy that *stronzo* got shot for, then your father has nothing to fear."

I thought back to the ugly man's words – *Tell your father my compliments to the chef* – and wondered if I should be worried.

"Your brother is judge, jury, and executioner – correct?" I asked.

Massimo shrugged. "Probably not the executioner."

Those words sent a cold chill through my heart – but I forced myself to sound angry rather than terrified. "I don't want him making a snap decision based on rumors or gossip."

Massimo gave me a small smile that was almost kind. "He is by far the most level-headed man I've ever met. Like I said, your father has nothing to fear... if he's innocent."

I looked at Massimo for a second more, then composed myself and walked past him down the stairs.

When I got back to the café, my father was sitting in a chair. He looked terrified. No wonder, seeing as Adriano was standing behind him like the grim reaper.

Don Rosolini glanced over at the bundle of clothes in my arms and raised one eyebrow. "She has no bag?"

"She's never gone anywhere before," Massimo explained.

"Hm. That's all you need?" the stranger asked me.

"I want something else before we go," I said.

"Go and fetch it, then."

"It's not a 'thing.' I want a *promise* – that you won't hurt my father," I said, surprising myself with my boldness.

That was too much for the Hothead.

"You are not in a position to be demanding *anything!*" Adriano snapped.

The handsome *mafioso* raised one hand, and Adriano fell silent once again.

It was something to behold – they might have been brothers, but it was like a master quieting his dog.

Massimo spoke up. "I already told her that if her father didn't join the plot against you, he'll be safe."

The *mafioso* looked at me. "I'll go one step further. I promise your father will be safe *even* if he conspired against me... so long as he admits the error of his ways and tells me *everything* he knows. AND if you go with me willingly. Fair enough?"

I swallowed hard. "...yes."

I glanced over at my father.

He looked terrified, but he remained silent.

I thought about bringing up what the ugly man had said to me –

Then remembered that these men were in the *Cosa Nostra*.

I wasn't going to gamble my father's life on the potentially empty promises of murderers.

"Nothing?" the *mafioso* said to my father, then turned back to me. "Perhaps he needs a bit more time to reflect. Are you ready?"

I leaned over and kissed my father's cheek. He grabbed onto my arm.

"It will be alright," Papa whispered. He smiled feebly, like he was attempting to convince me of something he didn't really believe.

I nodded and tried to be brave. Then I turned back to the *mafioso*. "I'm ready, Don Rosolini."

The handsome man gave me a devilish smile that was both seductive and frightening at the same time.

"My father was Don Rosolini," he said. "You can call me Dario."

# 5

Dario

She was the first thing I saw when I walked into the café.

Long brown hair spilling down her back in waves... a simple white dress...

Soulful brown eyes in the most innocent of faces.

I had been in prison four years, and only out for the last seven days.

Since my return, my brothers had tried to set me up with any number of high-priced escorts –

But I had resisted.

I told them it was too dangerous. That our enemies would try to get at me through a woman.

It was all a convenient excuse.

I didn't actually know *why* I had waited –

But now I knew.

I drank her in, taking in every inch of her.

Her breasts were on the small side, but shapely and firm beneath her modest dress.

Though her waist was tiny, she wasn't exactly thin – she had some meat on her, which is how I like them. I want my woman to be a *woman* when she's naked in my bed, not a stick figure.

Suddenly I wanted nothing more than to rip off her clothes and take her –

But it was her innocence that entranced me...

Those eyes that revealed everything she was thinking and feeling.

As soon as I saw her, I knew I had to have her.

She was scared of me – that much was plain.

But she was also surprisingly brave, willing to speak her mind.

Like when she protested, "I am no one's possession."

I liked that.

I liked it a great deal.

If she had been a shrinking little church mouse, I would have lost interest.

But she was like a spirited horse, begging to be broken.

There was only one moment I lost control, and then only slightly...

When she angrily said, "I am not a *whore* to be bargained over."

Her anger covered up her fear, which I could feel beneath her bravado...

But I could read her yearning even more clearly.

It radiated off her like heat –

And my own cravings responded in kind.

I walked over to her, grabbed her hair, and forced her head back to look at me.

I saw the terror in her eyes –

But also desire.

Desire to be taken.

A good little Catholic girl who would never lift a finger to sin...

But who wouldn't mind if a bad man did the sinning for her.

I leaned down to whisper in her ear so the others would not hear.

Just a little something for her and no one else – between the two of us.

A taste of what was to come.

Her hair smelled faintly like roses, and I wanted her all the more.

"You *will* be my whore," I whispered. "But *only* for me... and no one else."

Then I let her go.

Her look of shock – and desire – was priceless.

Part of me wanted to ravage her right there – to lay her back on a table and fuck her like an animal.

After four years in prison and never touching a woman...

To suddenly encounter the most alluring beauty I had ever seen in my life –

It was difficult, but I controlled myself.

Right now, her father was of strategic importance to the family.

And family came first.

I needed her father to reveal what was going on. I needed him to tell me *why* my enemy had been in his café that night.

That was why I made the promise not to take her virginity.

To gain both *his* trust... and hers.

Of course, I threw in the line about 'until she begs me' because it amused me...

But also because it let the old man know that his daughter was in danger if he didn't cooperate.

And because I wanted her to know *exactly* what was going to happen between the two of us.

I remembered an old line from a movie. A general spoke of conquering ancient Rome by gaining the people's love, not by threatening them with his army.

*I shall NOT violate Rome at the moment of possessing her.*

That was how I felt about this girl.

I could have easily taken her... physically overpowered her...

But I didn't want her body alone.

I wanted her *soul.*

I wanted her to moan – not from fear and pain, but desire.

I wanted to break her...

To feel her innocence turn to lust as I made her come, over and over.

I knew my brothers would disapprove. Niccolo in particular would rant and rave about how I was letting my cock do my thinking.

But the truth was, she was valuable as a bargaining piece.

I could have easily made the old man reveal all his secrets by having Adriano or Massimo torture his daughter in front of him...

But I would have sooner destroyed the *Mona Lisa*.

So I decided to steal the *Mona Lisa* and take her with me instead.

# 6

Alessandra

**M**y father was Don Rosolini.
*YOU can call me Dario.*
His words echoed in my mind as we left the café.
To me he was still *il Mostro*... the monster of Tuscany...
But maybe that was his father?
Perhaps the son was not as bad...
Then I reminded myself that he was a *mafioso* and had taken over his family after his father's death.
Whatever else he might be, Dario was still a criminal and a thug.
If only he hadn't been such a handsome one...
With such mesmerizing eyes...
We walked out into the cold night air. May in Tuscany is warm during the day but can be frigid at night.
I clutched my clothes to my chest, not wanting Dario to see my nipples beneath my dress.

To be truthful, I was not sure if the cold air was the only reason they were hard.

I silently chastised myself for my weakness and added one more thing to the list I would have to tell the priest at confession.

...although I would leave out the *details* of what Dario's gaze did to my body.

The three men led me to a beautiful black Mercedes sedan parked in the gravel outside the café. Adriano went to the driver's seat, Massimo took the front passenger seat, and Dario opened the back door for me.

"Such a gentleman," I said sarcastically.

He just smirked.

I settled into the leather seat and marveled at how soft and luxurious it was. I had never felt anything so sinfully delicious before.

Dario closed the door, then went around to the other side of the car and got in next to me.

Adriano started the engine – which sounded more like a purr than a roar – and backed the car out into the road.

"Your phone," Dario said as he held out his hand.

"What?"

"Your cell phone. Give it to me."

"Why?"

"I can't exactly have you contacting whomever you want, now can I?"

I grumbled and handed over my cell phone, which I had hidden inside my bundle of clothes.

It was my single luxury – the one thing I owned that was my connection to the outside world.

Adriano watched from the rearview mirror as Dario powered off the phone. "How *old* is that thing?! When did you get it, a decade ago?"

"I'm not as well-off as some other little rich boys in this car," I snapped.

Adriano flushed with anger. I was afraid my temper had gotten the best of me –

Until Massimo snorted in amusement.

I glanced over at Dario as he pocketed my phone. He was suppressing a smile, as well.

Adriano grumbled under his breath, but he went back to staring at the road.

We drove for half an hour. Very little was said. Dario and the others made no attempt at small talk, and I was content to stare out the window at the moonlight on the Tuscan countryside.

Long after midnight, we finally turned off a small two-lane road onto a paved drive. We drove for a couple of minutes through rows of cedars, then came to a ten-foot-tall wall with a massive iron gate. There must have been a camera or some sort of sensor because the gate opened slowly and the Mercedes glided through.

Another couple of minutes went by as we drove past gorgeous vineyards and orchards. The road gradually sloped upwards, and we finally broke through the greenery and reached an open space – at which point I gasped in amazement.

There was a gigantic mansion at the top of the hill, three stories tall with two large wings. Its slate roof gleamed under the moon, and warm yellow light shone from a quarter of the massive windows.

The house looked like something out of a fairy tale... although I wondered if it would be one with a happy ending.

The Mercedes pulled around a circular drive in front of the mansion, where four men dressed in black were waiting. They opened the car doors for us and murmured things like *"Padrone"* and *"Don Rosolini"* as we exited. Dario clapped one of the men on the shoulder and nodded to the others as we passed by.

For a moment I thought that perhaps these were the other brothers – but they stayed behind as the four of us walked up majestic marble steps to a pair of bronze doors at the front of the mansion.

One of the doors swung open to reveal a huge foyer decorated with crystal chandeliers.

A handsome man in a white dress shirt appeared in the doorway. He looked closer to Dario and Adriano in coloring and height, though he was clean-shaven. His eyes sparkled mischievously as he looked me up and down.

"Ah, so the master and his useful idiots return with a hostage!" he said in a joking voice. "At least she's a beauty – thank heaven for small favors."

He took my hand in his and kissed it.

He was charming, I would give him that.

"Niccolo Rosolini at your service, *bella*. I've arranged a room for you upstairs. Filomena here will escort you and show you to your chambers. Please stow your things and freshen up, then join us downstairs once you're finished."

He gestured to an old woman at the foot of a magnificent staircase. She had white hair and a face as wrinkled as a walnut, but she stood straight and tall in her black servant's dress. She also wore a kind smile.

"Follow me, child," she said with a Sicilian accent as she led the way up the stairs.

I glanced back to see where the others were going.

Adriano and Massimo were already walking into a parlor off the main foyer.

Dario was watching me with hungry eyes as I mounted the steps...

...and Niccolo waved his hand at me. "Shoo, shoo! We have questions for you, so don't dally too long!"

I turned and followed the old Sicilian woman up the stairs.

I wondered when Niccolo had learned about me. I finally decided Dario must have called while I was retrieving my clothes in my bedroom.

Filomena led me down a long hallway on the third floor, past paintings that looked like they belonged in a Renaissance museum. In fact, the entire house was *like* a museum, there was so much art.

Finally we reached a room with wooden doors, and Filomena opened them up.

Inside was the most palatial bedroom I had ever seen. The giant four-poster bed had a bedspread of purest white, which was turned down to reveal silken sheets and half a dozen pillows. There were more paintings in the room, along with an old stone fireplace.

Glass doors opened out onto a small balcony. Through the glass, I could see a gigantic lawn and a beautiful swimming pool that glittered in the moonlight.

I stared at everything in amazement. The room was ten times larger than my bedroom back home and far nicer than any place I had ever stayed in my life.

"Here is the bath," the woman said, leading the way to a door off the main room. "There are toiletries for you on the counter."

She flicked on a light, and I saw a modern marble countertop with glittering gold spigots. A new toothbrush sat in a box next to a fresh tube of toothpaste.

When I peeked inside the room, I spied an enormous bathtub with two showerheads in the ceiling.

I felt like I had died and gone to heaven.

"I'll wait for you in the hall," the old woman said as she turned to leave.

"Oh, I can find my way back," I said.

She smiled. "I'll wait for you in the hall. Don Rosolini's orders."

Then she stepped outside and closed the door.

I put my undergarments in a dresser, then hung my other clothes in a beautiful mahogany wardrobe.

I quickly used the bathroom, washed my hands and face, and stared at myself in the mirror.

No makeup... tousled hair...

I looked a mess.

I tried to make myself a bit more presentable – then remembered who I was making myself presentable *for*. A bunch of thugs and killers, that's who.

I should have tried to make myself *uglier* so they wouldn't touch me...

Although when I thought of Dario grabbing my hair back at the café, my entire body flushed with heat.

I quickly put it out of mind and walked back out into the hall.

Filomena was waiting for me.

"I'm ready," I said.

She smiled. "You're so pretty."

"Thank you," I said, blushing.

"Would you take some advice from an old woman?"

"Of course."

"Don Rosolini just returned home after four years in prison. To my knowledge, he has not had a woman to the estate since his arrival." She looked at me sternly. "*Never* be in a room alone with him. That is all I will say."

Her words chilled me to the bone...

But they also made me uncomfortably warm.

I thought of Dario not having touched a woman in four years...

And then I remembered his body pressed against mine back at the café.

I wondered what a brute like that, deprived of a woman's touch for so long, might do to her in the throes of lust...

I swallowed hard and nodded to indicate I understood the warning.

"Follow me," Filomena said. "I'll take you back to the Rosolinis."

We walked back down the hall and descended the staircase to the foyer.

I could hear voices behind the closed wooden doors of the parlor. One in particular sounded angry, almost on the verge of shouting.

Then Filomena knocked twice.

"Come in," said a muffled voice.

She opened the door for me and smiled – though there was something in her eyes that gave me pause.

"You'll be fine," she said in a quiet voice. "I'll see you tomorrow morning."

I nodded, then warily walked into the room –

And came face to face with the blond killer from the café.

## 7

I cried out and tried to back away from the assassin, but the door had already closed behind me.

I flattened myself against the door and peered up at him in terror –

But he just gazed down at me with his blue eyes and gave me an amused smile.

Niccolo yelled from 20 feet away. "Lars, for God's sake, get away from her! You're scaring the life out of the poor thing!"

"I'm not going to hurt you," he said to me in a deep, gentle voice.

"I said get away from her, not *talk* to her!" Niccolo shouted.

The blond man smiled at me once more, then walked across the room.

"Does this have to happen *now?*" Adriano asked angrily.

"She'll be here for the foreseeable future," Niccolo said, "and we can't very well keep Lars in the cellar, now can we? Best we get everything out in the open as soon as possible."

Niccolo swept over and took me by the arm, then walked me to a padded leather chair and gently forced me to sit.

"Don't worry, Lars is a teddy bear... unless you go up against the family, in which case you *should* be worried. Here, have a drink,"

Niccolo said as he poured a light brown liquid into a glass on the table beside me. "You could use a little something to put the blood back in your cheeks."

I looked around, frightened out of my mind. I was in some sort of a parlor, filled with leather chairs, dark wood paneling, and dim lighting. The scent of cigar smoke hung faintly in the air. It was all very masculine, like a private club within the house.

Lars strolled towards Adriano and Massimo. They stood off to the side with drinks in their hands.

"Is that the girl you saw?" Adriano asked.

"If it *wasn't* her, I don't think she would've nearly *fainted* when she saw him!" Niccolo shouted over his shoulder.

Lars just nodded to Adriano like *That's her.*

Dario sat at the far end of the parlor in a high-backed leather chair behind a massive desk. He looked like an emperor on his throne.

There were also two other men in the room I hadn't seen before.

One looked very similar to Niccolo but with slicked-back hair and a dour expression. He was the only person in the room in a three-piece suit with a tie.

The last one, the youngest of the lot, leaned against the wall. He was absolutely beautiful, with sensuous lips, a scruffy beard, and a mop of unruly hair. He could have been a world-famous pop star or movie actor, he was so gorgeous. When he caught my eye, he smiled and winked.

I turned away in embarrassment.

"Drink, drink," Niccolo said as he offered me the glass.

"No thank you," I mumbled as I stared at Lars, my mind racing fearfully.

Had they brought me here to kill me – like Lars had killed the man in the café?

But... why?

"It's only brandy – drink!" Niccolo ordered.

"She probably thinks you poisoned it," the dour man in the three-piece suit said.

"Don't *say* such things, Roberto – putting ideas in her head – *Madonn,*" Niccolo cursed, taking the name of the Virgin Mary in vain: *Ma-DON,* short for Madonna. He gulped half of the brandy in one swallow and set the glass back down beside me. "See? No poison, just brandy! And now my germs, yes, but the alcohol will kill all that. Drink, for God's sake!"

I took a sip, mostly to quiet him down and keep him off my back.

I coughed as the liquid burned in my throat.

"Are you alright?!" Niccolo asked in alarm.

"I get the feeling she's probably never had liquor before," Massimo said.

"It's not scotch or whiskey, it's *brandy!*" Niccolo exclaimed.

The giant shrugged. "She's rather innocent."

Niccolo looked down at me. "Have you had brandy before?"

I shook my head 'no' as I coughed some more.

"*Madonn,*" he cursed again. "A babe in the woods."

"And a beautiful one, at that," smirked the movie star leaning against the wall.

"Hands off, Valentino!" Niccolo threatened him. "Stick to banging the help!"

"I wasn't going to touch her," Valentino protested.

"You touch *anything* with a pussy," Niccolo snapped, then turned back to me. "Pardon my French."

"Not 'anything,'" Valentino said. "She has to at least *look* good."

"Oh, so you have standards – wonderful," Niccolo sneered.

For the first time since I had entered the room, Dario spoke.

"Alessandra is our guest," he said in his deep, smoky voice. "No one is to touch her. Understood?"

"I meant no disrespect," Valentino said somberly to Dario.

"Don't say it to *me* – say it to *her.*"

The gorgeous young man looked at me with wary eyes. "Sorry, *signorina.* I meant no disrespect."

I just nodded mutely.

"Wonderful, everyone's kissed and made up," Niccolo said – then started shouting at Dario. "What the hell were you thinking?!"

Niccolo was certainly the most theatrical and loudest person in the room. And he was the only one who seemed willing to go up against Dario. Everyone else paid the mafia don deference, but not Niccolo.

It would have been funny if they weren't a bunch of thugs and killers.

Dario replied in a slightly mocking tone of voice. "Her absence will loosen her father's tongue – or don't you agree, *consigliere?*"

*Consigliere –*

'Counselor.'

It was the term used for a mafia don's right-hand man, the godfather's most trusted advisor.

So Niccolo was not only Dario's brother... he was also the don's *consigliere* and the second-most powerful man in the room.

No wonder he joked and shouted while the others kept quiet.

"You could've done that without bringing her *here!*" Niccolo fumed. "Have you forgotten what line of work you're in?! A few threats would've worked nicely!"

Then Niccolo turned back to me hastily and said in a reassuring voice, "Not that we would have necessarily followed through on the threats, mind you."

'Necessarily' was the one word that stood out.

I understood all too well the implied threat.

But despite the danger I was in, I couldn't help but imagine the Seven Dwarves from *Snow White* when I looked around the room.

Instead of Grumpy, Doc, Bashful, and Dopey, however, it went something like this:

Adriano was the Hothead.

Massimo was the Bear.

Lars was the Blond.

Roberto was the Banker. I seriously would have expected him to work in finance, not in the mafia.

Valentino was the Loverboy, the ladies' man.

Niccolo was the Trickster –

But Dario was still *il Mostro.*

A chill ran down my spine every time I glanced over at him and saw him watching me like a predator looks at its prey.

I thought of Filomena's warning:

*Don Rosolini just returned home after four years in prison... he has not had a woman to the estate since his arrival... never be in a room alone with him.*

The way Dario looked at me, I understood all too well what she meant.

Suddenly Niccolo plopped down on the leather seat across from me. He smiled warmly. "Well, *bella,* you've certainly had quite the evening, haven't you? Have another sip of your brandy."

I choked down a bit more. I had no desire to run afoul of a *consigliere.*

"So... this fellow Lars dispatched so abruptly..." Niccolo shot the blond man a stern look like he was a very naughty boy indeed, then turned back to me. "Had you seen him in your café before?"

"No."

"Think hard. You're quite sure you'd never seen him before?"

"I'm sure."

"Do you think your father might have been acquainted with him?"

I thought of the ugly man and his final words to me:

*Tell your father my compliments to the chef.*

A flicker of fear passed through me – and it did not go unnoticed.

Niccolo leaned forward. There was something in his manner that reminded me of a serpent eyeing a baby chick. "What was that?"

"What was what?"

"That little twitch," he said, gesturing to his own face. "You had a thought just now. What was it?"

Perhaps it was the brandy that gave me courage...

Or perhaps I was just tired of being pushed around all evening.

Either way, I snapped, "I was wondering what kind of a man badgers a woman who's just seen someone *murdered* – and by someone else in the same room, no less."

Valentino snickered over by the wall.

But Niccolo... Niccolo gave me a cold smile that didn't reach his eyes.

"You're lying to me, *bella,*" he said quietly. "It would be a very good idea for you to tell me the truth."

As he stared into my eyes, I suddenly realized that the laughter, the shouting, the charm – it was all a façade.

Niccolo played the fool, but that was just to creep past your defenses...

Close enough to stab you with a stiletto.

I was frightened by the change in his mood – but I tried to hide it with more bluster.

"I want to go to bed. Or are you going to stop me from doing that?"

"No one here will stop you from doing *anything,* Alessandra," Niccolo purred. "Except leaving the estate. *That* is punishable by – "

Suddenly Dario's voice interrupted from the back of the room. "Niccolo."

It was a warning.

A command to back off.

Because I knew what the next word would have been:

*Punishable by death.*

There was a flash of anger in Niccolo's eyes... and then he was back to his regular old charming self.

"Of course, of course," he said as he settled back in his chair. "You must be exhausted, *bella* – you should go up and sleep. We can continue our talk in the morning."

I nodded and got unsteadily to my feet.

"Massimo, escort her to her room," Dario commanded.

"I can find my own way back," I protested.

"I know you can. Regardless, he's going with you."

I glared at Dario, but he just calmly stared back at me with those mesmerizing eyes.

It was hard to look away, but eventually I did.

The other eyes in the room were not nearly as enticing –

And some of them were a good deal more threatening.

Adriano with his anger...

Lars with his quiet amusement...

Roberto with his calculating gaze...

Valentino with his seductive smile...

And Niccolo with his piercing stare that sifted my lies like wheat.

"...fine," I said, wanting to get out of there as quickly as possible.

As I turned to leave, Massimo walked over to escort me to my room.

*"Sogni d'oro,"* Niccolo said with a touch of mockery in his voice.

'Sweet dreams.'

Literally, 'dreams of gold.'

Kept here against my will, in a house full of mafia thugs?

I was sure my dreams would be anything *but.*

I left the room as quickly as I could, with Massimo trailing behind me up the stairs.

When I got to my room, he stopped at the threshold.

"Sleep well," he said, then closed the door.

I heard a *click.*

After he left, I tried the doorknob...

...and discovered I was locked in.

I went to bed, but it was many hours before I could sleep.

Because even though I was locked in...

...*they* were not locked *out.*

# 8

I woke early the next morning – not because of the sunlight shining into my room, but out of habit.

I worked in my father's café six mornings of the week, and only got a reprieve on Sunday mornings because of mass – so I woke at the same time no matter how late I had gone to bed or how little sleep I had gotten.

But I had to admit, the bed was a dream... like floating on a cloud.

I rolled over on my side and considered sleeping in for the first time in years –

And that's when I saw it.

A dress that wasn't mine was hanging over a chair near the door.

A dress that *someone else must have put there while I was sleeping.*

I sat up in bed, as wide awake as if someone had doused me with ice-cold water.

I could imagine Dario standing above me, watching me sleep, and I shivered with fear...

Although something about the fantasy made me blush, too.

I was only wearing a negligee, and one of the straps had fallen off my shoulder.

What had he seen?

...and what might he have done if he hadn't made that promise to my father last night?

I heard his voice again in my mind:

*I give you my word, I will not take your daughter's virginity... until she begs me to do so.*

Then I remembered the second thing he had said, whispering it into my ear so that only I could hear it:

*You WILL be my whore. But only for me... and no one else.*

I shivered – and not entirely from fear.

There was a sliver of sinful desire within me, I will admit – but I would *never* beg him to do *that*.

If he kept true to his word, then I was safe.

*...if* he kept true to his word.

I got up out of bed and walked over to the dress.

It was quite beautiful – and modest, as well. Though made out of blue silk and thus far too expensive for me to ever buy, it was something I might have picked out for myself.

But I would not wear it.

I would not stand for him breaking into my room into the middle of the night to watch me as I slept...

And I would not give him the satisfaction of doing what he wanted.

I put on one of the other dresses I had brought, then brushed my teeth with the toothbrush Filomena had set out for me.

There was a hairbrush as well, and I did my best to tame my unruly locks.

I thought about taking a shower, but my stomach was rumbling. I hadn't eaten since the previous afternoon. The shock from the murder and everything that had happened after it had blunted my hunger, but now my appetite was back with a vengeance.

I sighed and went over to the door. Perhaps if I banged on the door, someone would come to let me out.

Just to see, I tried the doorknob –

And the door swung open.

I stood there, surprised... and then peeked my head out.

There was no one in the corridor, so I quickly slipped on my sandals and hurried to the stairs.

Though I could hear noises deep within the recesses of the house, there was no one in the foyer, either.

I thought about slipping out the front door and making a run for it – but then I remembered how big the estate was. I didn't stand a chance of escaping, so I just followed the sounds of voices – and the delicious smell of baking bread – until I found myself in the kitchen.

There was a woman there just a few years older than me. She was cute, with a short haircut, and she sang to herself as she whisked a large bowl of eggs.

I cleared my throat to make my presence known. "Ahem..."

The woman looked over and cried out. Then she clasped a hand to her chest and started laughing. "Oh, *signorina,* you startled me!"

"I'm sorry – "

"Don't be, don't be! You go back to bed and relax – I'll bring some food up to you right away!"

But the idea of Dario standing over me in my bedroom was something I no longer wanted to think about.

And the kitchen – with its ancient stone walls but modern appliances – was comforting. It felt more like home than anywhere else in the house.

Not to mention the smell of freshly baked bread was making my mouth water.

"Would you... mind if I stayed?"

The woman laughed again. "If you want – I could certainly use the company! My name's Cat – short for Caterina."

"Alessandra," I said shyly.

"A pleasure to meet you! What would you like to eat?"

"Is that fresh bread I smell?"

"Of course – right out of the oven!"

She went to a nearby cutting board and brought me a small loaf of *mugello,* one of the traditional breads of Tuscany. She also gave me with a knife, a plate, and a small dish with creamy butter. "That's from a dairy farm just down the road – you'll love it. Would you like some olives? Some fruit? Something to drink? If you tell me what you'd like, I'll fix it for you!"

Cat set me up with a *smorgasbord* of fruit, olives, and juices, then went back to her work.

"Are you the only cook?" I asked as I ate.

"Hardly! But Mariana was sick today, so I'm handling duties for breakfast. Usually it's the two of us through lunch, and then a separate staff handles dinner. We *used* to have many more people... until Don Rosolini died, God rest his soul."

She crossed herself.

I frowned. "When did *that* happen?"

"About three months ago."

"Dario was still in prison when he died?"

The very idea was so sad...

Even though I was afraid of the man and considered him a thug, no one should lose the chance to say goodbye to their parents at the end.

Cat turned around, her eyes wide. "How did you know about that? Did he tell you?"

"No, Filomena did."

Cat clucked. "That woman should know when to keep her tongue in her mouth."

I found that slightly funny since Cat was telling me about how the former mafia don had died – but I didn't bring up the irony.

"So... Dario was in prison when his father died?"

"Yes." Cat sighed heavily. "It was a sad day, a terrible day."

"But... why would that impact how many people work in the kitchen?"

Cat winced, like she was considering whether to say more.

Then the chatterbox side of her won out.

"Well, after the don died, a lot of people left."

"Why?"

"They were afraid."

I frowned. "Afraid of what?"

Suddenly a man's voice spoke behind me. "Gossiping *again*?"

I whirled around to see Valentino striding into the kitchen.

He smiled at me but passed right on by.

As he walked past Caterina, he grabbed her derrière and squeezed.

I don't know if he didn't think I saw –

Or if he just didn't care.

Caterina certainly did. She blushed bright red and looked at him like *What are you DOING?!*

But she had a gigantic smile on her face when she did it.

Valentino grabbed an apple out of a fruit bowl as he walked out of the room. "Don't give away *all* the family secrets, *capiche?*"

He gave Cat a wink, me a smile, and then he was gone.

She sighed heavily as he left – a lovelorn sound.

I looked between her and the doorway. "Are you and he...?"

She giggled, then grew very serious. "You can't tell anyone, alright?"

Suddenly I remembered what Niccolo had said last night:

*Hands off, Valentino! Stick to banging the help!*

I didn't want to tell her it wasn't exactly a secret, so I just nodded. "To my grave."

She giggled again and looked off into the distance dreamily. "It's been going on for two months now..."

"So... you're dating secretly?"

She smirked. "I wouldn't exactly call it 'dating.'"

"Are you going to marry?" I asked innocently.

If they were sleeping together, that was the only honorable end result, after all.

Caterina burst out laughing.

"ME? Marry a Rosolini? If *only*. I'd never have to work another day in my LIFE."

She sighed again, this time wistfully.

"But he's practically royalty, and I'm just a servant."

Then a shadow passed over Cat's face, along with a twinge of anger.

"Plus he'll never settle down. Not to mention that ALL Rosolini men are dogs."

Then she grinned and rolled her eyes back in her head.

"But they can FUCK. *Madonn,* can they fuck." She fanned herself with her hand. "Best sex of my life by FAR."

I blushed to hear her say it.

*No one* I knew talked like Cat –

But her words made me think of Dario again, standing over my bed as I lay there in my negligee... and the heat from my face seemed to travel to between my thighs...

Suddenly a voice *harrumphed* behind me.

I turned to see Filomena standing in the doorway.

Cat went red as a beet as the old woman walked over to the kitchen island where I was sitting.

Filomena gave Cat the evil eye, then turned to me.

Behind Filomena's back, Cat made a face like *Oh my GOD!* and stifled a laugh with her hand.

I had to focus on Filomena so I wouldn't burst out laughing, too.

The old woman scowled at me. "You are to accompany me to the patio at once."

"Yes, ma'am."

Filomena abruptly turned and started walking towards the doorway Valentino had exited.

Cat made another face like she couldn't believe how much trouble she was in – but found it hilarious all the same.

I frowned and choked back a laugh at the same time as I hurried to follow Filomena.

Cat waved and silently mouthed, *Come back later!*

I nodded and mouthed, *I will!*

No matter how much trouble she might be, I liked Caterina immensely and decided I would come visit her again as soon as possible.

Once I caught up with Filomena, the old woman said in her thick Sicilian accent, "You shouldn't associate with her. She's a common, vulgar girl – and a tramp."

"Mm," I said noncommittally.

The old woman stopped and turned on me. "Is your mother alive?"

I turned pale at the question.

I didn't want to answer... but I didn't feel like I could stay silent.

"...no," I finally said.

"When did she die?"

"When I was 12."

Filomena's entire demeanor changed, and her features turned from cross to sad.

She put her hand softly on my cheek.

The gesture was so loving... so motherly... that I felt tears well up unexpectedly in my eyes.

"Caterina is friendly, yes, but she is a bad influence," the old woman said in a kindly voice. "Her behavior is not suitable for a young lady. And *you* are a good girl – I know it. Just as I know your mother would want to keep you safe from bad influences."

I didn't respond. I still liked Cat – nothing would change that – but the old woman's tender concern was so touching, I didn't want to argue with her.

The old woman took away her hand and sighed. "Bad enough you must stay in this house of murderers..."

The words were jarring.

Just a second ago we had been talking about my new friend –

And now we were talking about being surrounded by killers.

"Why do you stay here, then?" I asked, trying to be delicate.

She smiled sadly. "Some of us have no good options, my dear."

Of everything she had said so far, those words sounded the most truthful by far...

...because they described my life perfectly.

# 9

Filomena led me through a stone hallway to a gigantic patio outside.

In the daylight, the Rosolini estate was astoundingly beautiful. Just beyond the patio was a gigantic lawn that led to a swimming pool lined with lemon trees. Beyond *that* was a topiary garden which gradually became vineyards.

But none of that was what caught my attention.

Instead, my eyes settled on the two men having a cup of coffee at an outside table: Niccolo and Roberto Rosolini.

Roberto wore another three-piece suit, although this time he didn't have a tie on.

Niccolo wore a white linen shirt and a pair of slacks. He looked casual and relaxed – but all I could think about was his sinister demeanor when he'd questioned me last night.

I wanted to run back inside –

But it was too late. Niccolo heard our footsteps and twisted around in his chair to see.

"Ah – *ciao, bella!* Have a seat, have a seat!" he said, gesturing to the empty chair to his left. Then he smiled at Filomena. "Thank you so much, *Signora,* for delivering our little lost lamb to us. *Grazie mille."*

The old woman smiled and bowed slightly at the neck. She gave me one last glance, but it was hard to read her expression – was it a warning? A look of sympathy?

Then she turned and went back into the house.

I sat down in my chair. Roberto watched me closely, as though trying to read my thoughts.

Niccolo, however, was back to his old charming self.

Only *now* I knew it was the mask he wore over his true nature.

This time I would be on my guard.

"Coffee? Tea? Juice?" Niccolo asked. "We have everything, and what we don't have, we can get. What would you like?"

I accepted some tea and buttered another piece of freshly baked bread.

"How did you sleep? Was the bed to your liking?" Niccolo asked with a smile.

"It was wonderful, thank you."

"Good. Alessandra... there's something I'd like to say to you."

My stomach dropped. I expected the sinister side of him to come out again – all veiled threats and dark innuendoes.

"...oh?" I asked, trying to control my fear.

"Look at your face!" he clucked. "Did I really scare you that badly last night?"

"Obviously," Roberto interjected.

"Quiet, you," Niccolo scolded his brother, then turned back to me. "I'd like to apologize for my conduct. I was under a great deal of stress... but that was no excuse for how I treated you. I was threatening when there was no need for it. Can you forgive me for scaring you so?"

I stared at him.

This was *not* what I had expected from a mafia *consigliere...*

...although maybe it was all part of the game.

The spider singing lullabies as it lured the fly into its web.

"...of course," I said hesitantly.

"I can tell you're less than convinced, so let me explain a bit more what actually happened. Our father died three months ago – "

"I'm sorry."

"Thank you, thank you. He was the patriarch of our family, and as you can imagine, losing him threw our entire world into chaos. We did not just lose our father – we lost our leader. Dario wasn't even *here* when Papa died. I might as well tell you since you're going to find out sooner or later – Dario was in prison at the time. Papa died unexpectedly and my brother didn't even get to say goodbye."

I already knew a good bit of that information from talking to Cat and Filomena, but two other questions formed in my mind almost immediately.

Niccolo anticipated them both.

"Dario went to prison on a racketeering charge involved with a bribery case," Niccolo said. "They nabbed a judge who was presiding over some of our family's business interests. As the oldest son, Dario took the fall for all of us. I know you were wondering – might as well come out with it and tell you straight.

"And no, our father did *not* die from a – how would you put it – a 'mob hit.' He had a heart attack. He was relatively young – 59 – and there was no warning, so it was quite a shock. He lingered for a couple of hours in the hospital, completely unconscious... and then he was gone."

"I'm so sorry," I whispered.

Part of me wondered whether anything Niccolo was telling me was the truth – but he genuinely seemed sad. There was real pain in his eyes as he talked about his father.

"Thank you, that's very kind. At least we got to say goodbye, even if he couldn't hear us or answer back. But the prison wouldn't even let Dario speak to him over the phone. Animals," Niccolo said angrily.

It was pretty ironic to hear a mafia *consigliere* call someone else an animal over a denied phone call... even if it *was* a very sad situation.

I kept that thought to myself, though.

"As a result of my father's death, the family business was thrown into disarray. That's when the wolves came out. There are numerous families like ours that run things all over Italy. When my father died, they saw an opportunity. We began to have troubles that hadn't occurred for decades: disputes with former partners, politicians on our payroll turning against us, sabotage in our operations... the truth is, the other families were probing us for weakness to see if they could wipe us out.

"Our uncle Fausto – my father's younger brother, and his *consigliere* for the last 25 years – took over half of the family's territory and business. My brothers and I kept the rest. We agreed unanimously that Dario would be the new head of the family, and he chose me as *consigliere* to handle things in his stead until he returned.

"But we've had our eyes on the wolves, tracking their plots to take us down. The man who was killed in your café last night was one such wolf. We know he worked for a rival family in Genoa, and we established his involvement in the firebombing of one of our warehouses.

"Needless to say, we found it *very* suspicious that he was in our territory just a week after Dario's return. Lars tracked him to your café and took care of him for us – but your father's café is in the middle of nowhere. We can't figure out *why* he would have gone there, other than to meet someone."

I stared at him in shock.

Niccolo had been extraordinarily open with me.

It might not have been the complete truth, but he had been under no obligation to tell me *anything*. I was their prisoner; prisoners don't get the luxury of asking their captors questions.

Niccolo seemed to read my thoughts.

"Quite a bit of information to digest," he said with a smile.

"...yes," I admitted.

"Well, Dario was quite cross with me after you left last night. He thought you deserved at least a partial explanation for my – as *he* called it – assholish behavior."

*Dario?!*

Dario was the one who had ordered Niccolo to apologize?!

That shocked me more than anything else I had heard so far.

Roberto spoke up. "So you see, we're trying to ascertain if

Umberto Fumagalli – the man from last night – knew your father, and why Fumagalli would be interested in him... or whether it really *was* just a coincidence that he walked into your café. Tell me – how long has your father had the business?"

"For as long as I can remember – at least since I was a baby."

"And how did he buy it? Do you know?"

"I don't..."

"How many customers did you have per day, would you say?"

I frowned. "What?"

Niccolo sighed. "Roberto is the head of business interests for the family. This is his great joy in life, asking nitpicky financial things. Humor him, if you will."

What came next was a strange barrage of questions: how much money we made in an average month. What our expenses were. If there was a mortgage on the property. Who our suppliers were for coffee and food. (A tiny market in Mensano.) If there were other members of the staff besides me and my father. (There weren't.) How much of our business was locals and how much was tourists.

Finally Niccolo waved off his brother. "Enough, Warren Buffett – your questions are boring poor Alessandra to death!"

"Whatever, Machiavelli."

Niccolo stood up abruptly. "Let me take you on a tour of the property, *bella,* before Roberto begins his stultifying line of questioning again. Hurry – I can see him breaking out the spreadsheets!"

Niccolo whisked me away from the table.

"I can't abide when he does that," he grumbled, then added facetiously, "Roberto doesn't seem to realize that not everyone shares his passion for accounting."

"Why did he call you Machiavelli?"

"Ah – it's a joke about my first name. You're familiar with the Renaissance philosopher Niccolo Machiavelli, author of the political treatise *The Prince?*" he asked as we entered the house and began to wind through the hallways.

"Yes, of course."

Machiavelli was known for his amoral advice to rulers: manipulate and lie in order to keep control over their subjects.

"Yes, well, all my brothers love to call me 'Machiavelli.' It used to annoy me – but if you're going to be a *consigliere*, there are worse nicknames to have."

"You and Robert look very much alike. Are you twins?"

"Yes, we are – but fraternal, not identical. Thank *God* I don't have an exact copy of his genes. The man has boring financial statements written into his DNA."

"There's something I don't understand..."

"Oh? And what is that?"

"You keep talking about your family and brothers... but Lars doesn't look like any of you."

Niccolo laughed. "Well, that would be because he's not related to us by blood."

"Does he work for you?"

"It's more than that. When Dario went off to prison, those wolves I spoke of? They tried to make sure my brother *died* in there, on more than one occasion. Lars was his best friend 'on the inside,' as they say, and saved Dario's life on two separate occasions. Lars finished his sentence six months ago, and Dario sent him to us to give him a job. He's actually become a seventh member of our family. He got to be around our father before he died, and Papa loved him as a son for saving Dario's life. Ever since everything went to shit, Lars has become our most trusted ally."

I frowned. "Even more than your uncle?"

Niccolo smiled wryly. "Do you *see* my uncle anywhere nearby?"

"Ah. Do you have any sisters?"

"No, alas. Mama had six boys. She always wanted a little girl, but she died when I was 18. Dario's the oldest, then Adriano, followed by Roberto and me, then Massimo. Valentino's the baby and a spoiled rotten little brat. But with a face like his, he gets anything he wants from the ladies."

I was surprised at how open Niccolo was being –

But from what I had seen, he *always* did everything for a reason.

And it was like he could read my mind.

"You might be saying to yourself right about now, 'My, but he's giving me a great deal of information!'" Niccolo said. "And yes, there's a reason. A couple of them, actually.

"You have questions, I'm sure. Hopefully I've answered the most pressing ones. Because there will be many others I *won't* answer. There are things this family does that are secret... and it would be best you not know too much about them. So don't ask."

My stomach tightened. Even though his tone was much lighter than the night before, the sinister implications were the same:

*Step out of line at your own peril.*

We reached the foyer of the mansion.

"In addition, there are parts of the house you're not allowed," Niccolo said. "Your bedroom is on the third floor. Anything up there is fine. So is the ground floor, unless the door is locked. In that case, don't pry. But the second floor of the eastern wing – "

He pointed to the right side of the building.

" – is completely off-limits. Don't go beyond the staircase. Ever. Understood?"

His voice wasn't threatening this time, but it *was* firm.

I was immediately curious what was up there and why it was forbidden – but I just nodded. "Understood."

"Good." He smiled. "Feel free to roam the property, but don't go beyond its boundaries, either. If you need anything, just ask."

"How long will..."

I wanted to say, *How long will you be keeping me here,* but I thought that sounded a bit hostile.

And Niccolo *had* gone out of his way to be...

Well...

*Less* threatening.

"...um, how long will I be staying?"

"Still to be determined."

"I'll need to wash my clothes at some point."

Niccolo waved his hand dismissively. "Just give them to Filomena

– she'll take care of it. We should probably get you some new things to wear, as well."

"Why bother?" a deep voice said behind me. "She wouldn't wear them anyway."

My heart skipped a beat.

From fear –

...and maybe something else, as well.

I whirled around to see Dario. He had entered the foyer as silent as a cat, and was staring at me with an irritated look.

"I don't take gifts from men who intrude on my privacy," I snarled.

Dario frowned. "What are you talking about?"

"The dress!"

He gave me a look of disgust, like *I know THAT.* "I'm talking about the 'intrude on your privacy' nonsense."

Now I was furious. Just because he could kidnap me and use me as a hostage didn't mean he could gaslight me. "You entered my room while I was *sleeping* – "

"I had a *servant* leave it," he snapped. "A servant *girl,* as a matter of fact."

Oh.

I blushed bright red.

Now that he said it, a servant made far more sense.

It wasn't like a mafia don would silently tip-toe into my room to leave a dress.

I felt stupid...

But my embarrassment quickly gave way to anger.

Yes, I had jumped to conclusions – but only because I had felt so unsafe from the night before.

And they weren't exactly the most outlandish conclusions, given everything he'd already done and said.

Apparently Dario didn't see it that way, because he shook his head in contempt. "What do you take me for?"

"A kidnapper? A criminal? A man who said he would make me his *whore?*" I nearly shouted.

Niccolo's eyebrows shot up. He looked intensely uncomfortable, like he would have rather been *anywhere* else at that moment.

Dario walked towards me, every step a threat.

I backed away slightly, overwhelmed and frightened by his size and his murderous stare.

*You idiot!* I cursed myself silently. *You KNOW what he is – why would you say something so STUPID?! Why would you provoke him?!*

He got right up next to my body and towered over me.

I began to breathe faster as I stared up into his angry eyes.

"If you're not careful," he said in a whispering snarl, "I might decide to go ahead and start my plans early."

Because he was so close, I could smell his scent again – that subtle, expensive cologne he wore.

I could feel the heat radiating off his body.

I stood there, mouth open, almost hypnotized.

Then he turned and walked away without a word, leaving me standing there stunned...

...and more than a little bit turned on.

Niccolo waited until Dario disappeared from the foyer, then he said to me, "Well, YOU certainly know how to poke the wild beast, don't you?"

"It's not my fault," I pouted.

"Not your *fault?!* Not your FAULT?!" Niccolo said with an incredulous laugh, then began to mimic me in a high-pitched voice. "'A kidnapper? A criminal? A man who said he was going to make me his – '"

"Alright, so I shouldn't have provoked him," I interrupted. "I won't make the same mistake twice."

"You're lucky you got to make it *once*. Believe me when I tell you this, *bella:* I don't know *anyone* else who could have spoken to Dario like that and lived to tell the tale."

I didn't know how I felt about that.

On the one hand, Niccolo seemed to be suggesting that Dario had a certain weakness for me...

...and then he had to throw in some more insinuations about murder.

I didn't want to think about any of it, so I just ignored it.

As soon as Niccolo said the last bit about 'living to tell the tale,' he began to walk away from me.

"Where are we going now?" I asked as I followed in his footsteps.

"*We?* There is no 'we' – *I'M* going to go prepare for some meetings. *You* can do whatever you like except for come with me – or go into the second floor of the east wing. Dinner will be served at 8 in the dining room."

"What am I supposed to do until then?"

"Anything you like – or nothing at all! Just don't go into the areas we talked about... and don't try to leave the grounds," he said with a smirk.

With that, Niccolo disappeared around a corner and left me all alone.

# 10

The first thing I did was go looking for a telephone.

Dario had confiscated my cell phone, so I was without any way to contact the outside world – but my father still had a landline in the café. If I could find a telephone in the mansion, I figured I could call Papa to make sure he was alright.

I could have asked Niccolo, but I was almost certain he would have said 'no.'

As long as I didn't ask, I could plead ignorance. After all, they hadn't *explicitly* told me I couldn't call anyone.

Better to ask forgiveness rather than permission.

I poked around until I found an open study with a telephone on the desk. I was a bit intimidated by all the buttons and lights on the console, but I picked up the phone and listened.

There was dead silence.

I pushed a button on the console, hoping that would work –

When suddenly a woman's voice spoke in my ear.

*"Hello, how may I direct your call?"*

Heart thudding in my chest, I slammed down the receiver.

After that, I didn't feel safe staying inside the mansion.

And whether it was Filomena's warning or just not wanting to bother her while she worked, I thought I should leave Caterina alone.

I had nothing else to do, so I began to walk the grounds.

They were enormous.

There was an old horse stable made of stone set apart from the house, and it had been turned into a twelve-car garage. Inside were numerous black and silver Mercedes, a couple of Range Rovers, and several sports cars, including a midnight blue Bugatti.

The swimming pool was beautiful and pristine, with a marvelous tile mosaic under the crystal-clear waters – but the temperature was a bit cool for swimming.

Plus I didn't have a swimsuit. I was sure one would have magically materialized if I'd asked... but I shuddered to think what a bunch of *mafiosos* would give me. Probably tiny scraps of cloth that barely covered anything.

The gardens were amazing, with bushes and shrubs cut into all sorts of interesting shapes. There were also gorgeous patches of flowers in a dozen different colors.

Everywhere I went, there were young men in their 20s keeping guard. All of them had guns slung over their shoulders – either shotguns or some sort of military-looking rifle.

All of them were polite and greeted me with *"Ciao, signorina."* There were a few lingering stares but nothing more.

I guess Dario's instructions that I not be touched had filtered down to the foot soldiers.

But their presence made me nervous, so I went off to a field where no one was around.

As I walked, I looked for a route to make my escape. I didn't like being jailed here, no matter how luxurious the cell.

Being the Rosolinis' prisoner – especially Dario's – filled me with anger and dread. I desperately wanted to get back home to my father, so I began to study the grounds and see if there was a way to leave undetected.

As I was walking, movement on the ground suddenly caught my eye.

I looked down and my heart stopped.

Coiled on the ground not four feet away was a viper.

There are only two poisonous snakes in Tuscany, but the aspic viper is by far the most common – and the most dangerous.

People could die from their bites. It didn't happen often, but it *did* happen.

I was standing there, terrified, frozen in place –

When suddenly I heard a distant CRACK –

And the snake's head exploded.

I shrieked and stumbled backwards, then looked behind me.

At first I didn't see where the gunshot could have come from – there was no one in the field –

And then I looked at the mansion, which was over 600 feet away.

Someone waved to me from one of the balconies on the third floor.

I couldn't tell much about his face – but I could see the sun glinting off his golden hair.

Lars.

I saw him motioning me towards the house with a big motion of his arm.

I dutifully walked back. I was a bit glum that my every move was apparently being tracked...

But on the other hand, I didn't care to stumble across any more poisonous snakes.

Lars met me halfway, in the middle of the field near the swimming pool. There was a curving set of stairs directly from the third floor to the ground level, which is how he reached me so quickly. There was a massive sniper rifle slung over his shoulder.

"You have to be careful out here," he said with a smile. His Italian was excellent, though he still had an indistinct European accent that stood out from everyone else's. He didn't sound Swedish, but he *definitely* didn't sound local.

"You shouldn't stray so far from the house," he continued in a friendly tone.

"Or what, you'll shoot me?" I snapped.

Ordinarily I would have gone out of my way not to anger him – but I was still afraid from the viper, and adrenaline was coursing through me. That's probably why I was so bold.

He just chuckled. "No, I'd have to sling you over my shoulder and carry you back, and you might not like that so much."

I looked at Lars warily. Of all the people I had encountered, he was the one I feared the most – because of what I had seen him do in my father's café.

The others were frightening in their own right. Adriano had a terrible temper, and Niccolo concealed a sinister side beneath his friendly chatter –

Actually, I take that back.

I feared Dario the most.

He was like a silent wolf, always watching me like he might devour me at any second.

However, I also had other feelings for Dario that partly offset my fear.

When he was close to me, my body reacted in ways I had no control over.

Lars was very handsome, yes, but I felt nothing for him. And every time I looked at him, all I could picture was him killing the man in the café.

He seemed to know exactly what I was thinking, because he said, "You have nothing to fear from me."

"Riiiight. I have *nothing* to fear from the man tracking me with a gun."

"I was ordered to keep you safe. Which, you must admit, I just did."

"Yes, but the snake's not the *only* thing I've seen you shoot."

"The man last night was a snake, as well. Just a different type."

"Let me guess – you were protecting me *last night,* too," I said sarcastically.

"No. I was protecting the family." He meant the Rosolinis. "Although, one could argue that I protected you by walking out of the café after it was over."

I trembled slightly. It was true – he could have killed me easily. And it probably would have been in his best interest to do so.

The thought made my blood run cold.

"Why *didn't* you kill me?" I asked quietly.

"I thought the snake was a bigger threat," he joked.

"You know what I meant. Why didn't you shoot me last night?"

"Why would I?"

"I was the only witness – and you looked right at me. I could have identified you to the police."

"I don't kill women or children. Ever."

"What if they ordered you to?" I asked, gesturing with my head towards the house.

"They wouldn't."

"That's a first," I muttered. "*Mafiosos* not willing to kill someone."

"They're different than you think."

"How so?"

"You should ask Niccolo or Dario. It's not my place to talk about the family's business. But let's just say that they aren't your ordinary, everyday *mafiosos*," he said, gently mocking my choice of what to call them.

"Hm," I said as I walked with him back towards the house. "Are you Swedish?"

"I am."

"Niccolo said you saved Dario's life twice in prison."

"I did."

"And that's why they trust you?"

"It is."

"Were you in the military, too? In Sweden?"

"I was."

"That's why you're such a good shot?"

"Partly."

"You're talkative, aren't you?"

He smiled again. "I would talk more, Alessandra, if I knew my secrets were safe with you."

"What secrets?"

"Who I am. What I've done. Who I work for."

"I already know those things."

"And I see no need for you to know more."

"Then why bring me here?"

"It wasn't *my* choice."

I remembered how Niccolo had complained to Dario last night about him bringing me back to the house.

I also knew that Niccolo was the only one who dared contradict his brother.

No one else would cross Dario...

But Lars had just revealed that not everyone else agreed with Dario's choice.

Probably *none* of them did.

"Why *did* he bring me back here?" I asked.

Lars shrugged. "Dario does what he wants. But I think you know the risk he's taking by bringing you here. You've seen a great deal. You could say the wrong things to the wrong people."

"And *then* you would shoot me."

Lars shook his head. "Not me."

"Who, then?"

He looked at me silently, and I knew the awful answer:

Dario.

Dario would be the one to end my life if I stepped out of line.

He really *was* a monster.

I was suddenly more terrified than any point since the murder last night. Even the snake had not filled me with such fear.

Lars saw my reaction and tried to backpedal.

"Just stick to the house and the nearby grounds, Alessandra," he said quietly. "Do what you're told, and you'll get to go home soon enough."

"When?"

"I don't know. Just be careful," he said, and this time he didn't smile. "There are vipers everywhere."

I knew he wasn't just talking about animals in the grass.

With that, he climbed the stairs to take up his post again...

...and I went back inside, too afraid to do anything else.

# 11

I was too stressed out by my talk with Lars to eat lunch, so I was ravenous when 6PM finally rolled around and it was time to get ready for dinner.

I took a shower and used the amazing scented soaps and shampoos lining the tub. I thought about using the blow dryer on the countertop to dry my hair, then decided against it. It could just dry naturally, though that would probably take hours.

After all, I wasn't going to a beauty contest.

I was going to dinner with a bunch of criminals and killers...

One of whom would apparently murder me if need be.

I was about to slip on one of my own dresses, then saw the one the servant girl had left while I was sleeping.

It was still draped over the chair. No one had moved it.

I wondered if Dario had commanded the servants *not* to move it until I had worn it.

Part of me rebelled and wanted to throw it out the window –

But I also remembered Lars saying *Not me* when I asked who would kill me if the time ever came.

"Don't make the monster any more angry than he already is, Alessandra," I cautioned myself.

I slipped on the dress, though I gritted my teeth while I did it.

It was actually extremely nice, far more luxurious than anything I had ever worn before.

The blue silk was like a constant caress on my skin... and it was cut modestly, revealing no more than my own clothes.

But I resented it.

It felt like a shackle around my neck, one more chain binding me to this beautiful prison I couldn't leave... and to the jailer who held my life in his hands.

Still, my fear was enough that I wore the dress down to dinner.

I didn't know where the dining room was, but I found it by listening for Niccolo's animated speech as he talked and laughed with his brothers.

When I walked through the doors, everyone in the room looked at me and fell silent.

That is, until Niccolo said, *"Madonn,"* under his breath.

All the brothers (and Lars) were seated around the table, three on each side. Dario sat at the head of the table on the other end of the room.

His eyes flashed at the sight of me – and his eyes dropped to the dress.

He didn't smile, exactly, but his gaze was softer when he looked me in the eyes again.

Valentino whistled.

Massimo gently smacked him on the back of his head.

"What?! She looks beautiful!" Valentino protested to the others. "Don't tell me *you're* not all thinking it, too!"

I blushed.

"Sit, Alessandra," Niccolo said from his spot at Dario's right hand. "We saved the seat of honor for you."

Roberto, who was closest to me, stood up and pulled out the empty chair at the far end of the table from Dario. Then he pushed it underneath me as I sat.

"Thank you," I said quietly.

"Thank you for joining us, *bella*," Niccolo said. "And punctual, too!"

"Yes, well, you should congratulate yourselves," I said. "I've never seen six Italian men be on time for *anything.*"

Everyone chuckled except for Dario.

Although he smiled... just barely.

"It's Lars," Niccolo joked. "His Swedish-ness cancels out our perpetual Italian lateness and makes us all on time."

"I thought it might be *il Duce* at the head of the table there," I said, nodding at Dario, "making the trains run on time."

My joke was met with silence.

For a second I was worried I had made a horrible misstep –

And then the entire room burst into laughter.

Even Dario grinned.

"Mussolini Rosolini," Niccolo rhymed.

"What can I say," Dario said. "It's good to be dictator."

The brothers laughed, but his little joke set my teeth on edge.

Dario *was* the dictator of the house...

And his boot was firmly on my neck, just as my life was in his hands.

I tried to ignore my feelings of resentment, but they slowly built throughout dinner.

Perhaps a little of my boldness increased with the delicious red wine. I might have had a little *too* much with dinner, which was marvelous. I had never eaten so many wonderfully prepared foods. Servants came and went in silence, whisking away plates and setting down new dishes:

Bowls of *pappa al pomodoro,* tomato soup made of sun-ripened Tuscan tomatoes.

*Tagliolini al tartufo*, long ribbons of pasta drizzled in melted butter, garlic, and shaved black truffle.

*Potato tortelli,* pasta filled with mashed potatoes and seasoned with garlic and sage.

*Bistecca alla Fiorentina,* tender steak seared with spices and salt.

By the time we had a heavenly *tiramisu* for dessert, I was stuffed –

And more than a little bit tipsy.

Which meant my tongue was a bit looser than it should have been.

I'd said very little during dinner. Talk had consisted mostly of business dealings that didn't interest me in the slightest. Lots of extremely mundane things involving shipping and bribing local officials.

Thankfully I didn't have to listen to talk about people being 'whacked.'

There were also a number of off-color jokes you would expect amongst a bunch of twenty-something men.

But I got the sense that if conversation veered too close to something involving the *true* 'family business,' Niccolo rapidly shut it down.

Which irritated me.

It was all a show – a façade meant to pretend everything was normal when it most decidedly was *not.*

I was *forced* to be here.

I could not leave.

One of the men at the table had killed someone last night right in front of me.

And he had let it be known that my life was under threat by the man sitting directly across from me...

...the same one who had said he would make me his whore.

*Bastard,* I thought to myself angrily on more than one occasion.

What annoyed me more than anything was how *handsome* he was.

How powerful.

How rich and mysterious and dangerous.

There I sat in his house, eating his food, wearing the dress he had given me...

His prisoner.

I was furious.

I *hated* him.

Partly because he was this oppressive, villainous figure in my mind...

...and partly because I couldn't take my eyes off him.

His gorgeous face...

His broad shoulders...

The tattoos visible at the open neck of his dress shirt...

Dario mostly seemed to ignore me, although every so often he would catch me looking at him. His eyes would meet mine and he would hold my gaze.

The first couple of times, I looked away guiltily when he caught me –

But as I drank more wine, I began to see it as a challenge. I would keep my eyes locked onto his, almost as though I was daring him to look away first.

But he never did.

His eyes would drink me in... and I would begin to feel hot...

Almost like I could tell he was undressing me in his mind...

Until finally I would look away, uncomfortable with how my body responded to his gaze.

None of this improved my mood...

And it all came to a head at the end of dinner.

"I would like to leave the grounds tomorrow," I announced. "Temporarily."

"What for?" Niccolo asked.

"I want to go to church."

It was actually a ruse to get off the estate. I didn't care so much about going to church as I did contacting my father –

Or maybe escaping altogether.

"There's a private chapel in the western wing of the house," Dario said. "Go there."

"I can't say confession there," I protested.

Dario leaned back in his chair and smirked. "What horrible sins have you committed, exactly?"

"None as bad as yours, I'm sure," I snapped.

I immediately regretted it.

*You FOOL!* I thought. *What are you DOING?!*

Everyone's eyes immediately went to Dario.

His smirk didn't fade, though.

If anything, he seemed amused by my challenge to his authority.

"I'm sure if you ask, God will forgive you," he said in a mocking voice.

I replied with my own brand of mockery. "Perhaps you don't understand how these things work, having never set foot in a church before, but I need to speak with a priest."

"The priests around here are worse than us *mafiosos* you so despise. Trust me, you'll be better off in the chapel."

"I want to – "

"No," he interrupted sharply. "Now stop asking."

I narrowed my eyes and sneered, "But I really *should* do penance for all the hatred I feel in my heart."

"Hatred is nothing. Be more concerned about what you feel between your thighs."

The way he stared me straight in the eyes when he said it –

The way he made me *blush* –

I hated him all the more.

"Trust me, lust is the *least* of my sins," I snapped.

"Probably true, considering all the lies you tell."

I stared at him. "What?!"

"You don't want to go to church to confess anything. You want to contact your father like you attempted to do today on the phone."

So he knew.

"All the phones in the house go to a central switchboard," Niccolo explained gently. "The woman in charge of the system said that someone tried to make an outbound call this afternoon. When they didn't answer her question, she just assumed it was you."

I blushed hard.

I felt like a fool.

I had thought I'd been so stealthy –

And they all knew.

They were *laughing* at me behind their backs.

The stupid little peasant girl...

I got up from the chair with as much dignity as I could muster. "Then I guess I'll just go to the chapel... in order to get away from the asshole in *here*."

It was one of the few times in my life I had cursed.

I felt a certain pang of guilt –

But it was also *oh* so satisfying.

Dario smiled coldly. "Careful, little girl. God may forgive you... but I forgive *nothing*."

"I would expect nothing less from the devil," I said, and turned and walked out of the room.

# 12

I fumbled my way through the western wing of the mansion, tipsy and unsure of where I was, until I finally reached the chapel at the far end.

A lot of the house was new and updated – the bathrooms, the kitchen, the study. But other parts of the mansion were hundreds of years old: the stone walls, the arched ceilings, the marble stairs.

The chapel was part of the building that was a holdover from the distant past...

And it was more beautiful than I could have imagined.

The door was a massive slab of oak carved with scenes from the Bible: Adam and Eve, Noah and the Flood, the Crucifixion. It felt entirely possible that some Renaissance artist had made it 500 years ago.

As I placed my hand on the door and pushed, it creaked open, revealing a world lost in time.

The room itself was relatively small compared to the grand halls in the rest of the mansion, but as a result it felt snug and comfortable.

There were only two sources of illumination: the light from the hallway, and the moon filtering through a stained glass window at the far end of the room. Even in the dim light, the room struck me with its beauty. I promised to return the next day to see what it looked like with the sun streaming through the colored glass.

I felt along the wall for a light switch and found nothing.

I looked up at the ceiling and realized there were no light fixtures. However, there *were* several candelabras at the far end of the room sitting atop a table.

I carefully walked down the shadowy center aisle until I reached the candelabras. A box of matches sat beside them on the table, and I lit the candles one by one until the entire room was glowing with light.

Now that I could see more, I gasped at the domed ceiling. It was painted with angels and clouds so beautiful that they should have been in a far grander church.

The stone walls were hung with tapestries, their faded colors depicting the twelve stations of the cross.

I stood there in awe... until I heard footsteps behind me.

I whirled around to see Dario in the doorway. He had paused at the threshold and was watching me.

"Are you afraid you'll burst into flames if you come in?" I taunted him.

He smirked, then walked into the chapel and looked down at his hands as if examining them. "No flames of hell yet."

"Give it time."

He chuckled and looked around the room. "I haven't been in here since... I don't know when."

"Ever?"

"As a child, I used to come in here to pray... but that was a long time ago."

I could imagine him as a small boy sitting in the dark wooden pews, looking up at the angels... and the image softened my heart.

"Do you like it?" he asked.

"It's beautiful," I admitted.

"Good. Then you won't need to leave the estate."

Our argument at the dining room table came flooding back, along with all my resentment at being his prisoner.

"I need to go to church," I said stubbornly.

His eyes flashed with anger. "You *need* to OBEY me."

"'Wives, submit to your husbands as to the Lord,'" I said, quoting Ephesians. Then I added mockingly, "You mean like that?"

His smile was dangerous. "Minus the husband and wife part... yes."

I stood tall and looked him directly in the face. "I'll do what you order me to, because you'll kill me if I don't. But submit to you? *Never.*"

Maybe it was the wine that made me so brave.

Maybe I was emboldened by the fact that we were in a chapel.

I thought that Dario would at least respect the fact that we were standing in a holy place.

I was wrong.

He grabbed the back of my hair again like he had last night and pulled gently, forcing me to look up at him.

My heart beat rapidly with fear –

But excitement, too.

The feel of his body against mine as he stared down at me –

The anger in his face –

It was both frightening and... I'm ashamed to say it... erotic.

"I told your father I would not take your virginity until you begged me," he whispered hoarsely. "What I *didn't* say was that I will do whatever else I *like* with you... and TO you. I *will* make you my whore... and when the time comes, you *will* beg me to take you."

My entire body trembled –

And then he leaned over and kissed me.

I was too shocked to do anything but stand there.

I had kissed a couple of boys in years past – awkward moments behind the school building.

Those were *nothing* like this.

He was *so tall...*

So *powerful.*

His lips were soft and warm on mine – and I felt the tickle of his neatly trimmed beard on my skin.

At first I did nothing as his lips pressed softly against my mouth –

And then I *mmmphed!* and pushed as hard against his chest as I could.

But his other arm – the one not tugging at my hair – looped around my waist and pulled me effortlessly against him.

My soft curves pressed against his hard, muscular body.

The harder I fought, the harder he pulled me against him –

And the harder he kissed me –

Until he suddenly dipped me backwards.

I grasped his broad, powerful shoulders by instinct, trying not to fall –

And in that moment, I gave in.

I surrendered...

And it was bliss.

The softness of his kiss, growing firmer by the second –

The tug of his hand in my hair –

It was too much for me.

I felt his tongue softly touch my lips...

And I opened my mouth to him.

I opened *myself* to him.

We seemed to stay like that for an eternity...

Him holding me in his arms, swept off my feet –

Our tongues softly touching in the most sensual feeling I had ever experienced.

I was not aware of it consciously, but heat filled my entire body –

My breasts –

Between my thighs.

I couldn't think straight. All I knew is that I wanted more –

And then it was over.

He pulled me back up on my feet and broke off the kiss –

And with a smirk, he left me standing there filled with longing.

*"Ciao, bella,"* he whispered in his smoky voice, then strolled out of the chapel as I stood there, trembling with desire, aching for him to come back and do it all over again.

# 13

Dario

She was the most delicious thing I had ever tasted.

There was the wine on her tongue and lips...

But beneath the wine was a sweetness I had never encountered with any other woman. And there had been many in my lifetime.

She struggled at first, trying to push me away –

But she was weak as an infant, and I easily overpowered her...

Until she gave in.

*That* was the moment I wanted.

*That* was the moment I had been waiting for.

I felt her resistance fade...

And suddenly she was melting into me.

When I dipped her back and she grabbed my arms, my victory was complete.

But it wasn't just conquering her...

It was the sweetness of her.

The absolute purity and innocence of her kiss.

I had never experienced anything like it.

I was hard as iron within seconds –

And I wanted nothing more than to tear that dress off her and possess her – to thrust deep inside her and hear her cries of ecstasy –

But I knew that if I went too far, she would rebel.

She must surrender to me completely before I took that final step.

She had to *beg* me to take her.

But after four years of not touching a woman, I was nearly overcome with desire.

Imagine four years of never tasting sugar – no grapes, no oranges, nothing –

And then you bite into the most delicious strawberry that God ever made.

I knew my lust would overpower me if I didn't walk away at that moment.

And so I did the hardest thing I had ever done with a woman:

I stopped and walked away from her.

The blood pounded in my veins –

My cock throbbed, hard as steel –

But I knew it was the only way.

*I shall NOT violate Rome at the moment of possessing her.*

She would beg me soon enough...

And *then*...

THEN I would possess her, body and soul.

# 14

Alessandra

I did not sleep well at *all.*

After I first got in bed, I relived that moment over and over –

Every second of Dario grabbing me, kissing me, *taking* me –

Every touch, every taste, every sensation.

My thoughts eventually turned to worse things.

Like how it would feel if he pulled my dress up past my thighs, the silk sliding across my skin...

How it would feel if he touched me between my legs, which throbbed hot and wet and full of lust.

Over and over again, I forbid myself from thinking such things...

And over and over again, the thoughts still intruded.

I tossed and turned for hours before sleep finally came –

And even *then* I had no relief.

In my dreams, he came to me over and over.

Sometimes gentle...

Sometimes a brute.

Either he would slide my negligee off me...

Or he would rip it to shreds.

He would gently make love to me...

Or take me like an animal, frenzied and wild.

And every time he did, I cried out as he entered me –

Hating him –

And wanting him even more –

Until I woke in the morning, my sheets tangled around me.

I rolled over onto my side and felt immense shame.

A *mafioso* had forced himself upon me, and all I could do was quiver and want more.

Every sermon I had ever listened to, every warning about lust came flooding back into my brain.

I felt like I was in danger of going to hell for my desires.

This was no ordinary man I was fantasizing about.

He was a criminal.

A thug.

A murderer.

A mafia don.

The fact that I wanted him against my will...

The fact that my body responded so powerfully to his touch, betraying me...

What did that say about my soul?

I felt tainted by sin...

And for the first time since I had begun scheming, I wanted to go to church not just to escape the grounds and contact my father, but to unburden my soul and ask for forgiveness.

I was in danger of hellfire for the feelings that Dario Rosolini inspired in me...

And I would do *anything* to be rid of those feelings once and for all.

I dressed quickly, not in the silk dress he had given me, but in one of the dresses I had brought from home.

I knew he would not allow me to leave.

My mind kept returning to my mistake with the telephone yesterday. I knew I would have to gather more information if I wanted to escape the grounds.

But how?

...Cat.

Caterina would tell me what I needed to know. I was sure of it.

I made my way down to the kitchen. It was early enough that the house was barely stirring. I walked quietly, not wanting to encounter *anyone* – least of all Dario.

I entered the kitchen, but no one was there.

However, there were signs that Cat was nearby.

There were sliced strawberries on a cutting board...

And fresh dough set aside to be kneaded.

Plus her cell phone sat on a nearby counter. It was unlocked, like she had been looking at it before she disappeared.

I glanced around the kitchen. She didn't seem to be anywhere nearby.

She might know that I wasn't allowed to use my own phone... so I figured *Ask forgiveness, not permission* was the best policy.

I hastily grabbed the phone, opened Google Maps, and typed in *Church near me.*

The map zoomed in to a tiny village. I pinched the screen to shrink it, so I could figure out where I was in relation to the town –

But no matter how much I zoomed out, there was no sign of the Rosolinis' mansion. Just an empty green space.

I frowned as I tried to figure it out –

And then suddenly I heard a muffled cry, like someone sobbing into a pillow.

It was coming from inside the pantry, just ten feet away.

The wooden door was almost completely closed... but there was a tiny crack.

There were muted cries coming from within...

But it didn't sound sad.

It sounded...

*Passionate.*

I closed Google maps, replaced the phone on the counter, and slowly crept to the door, my heart thudding in my chest.

Then I peered through the crack in the almost-closed door.

What I saw shocked me –

And aroused me almost as much as Dario kissing me the night before.

Inside the pantry, Valentino was making love to Cat.

Well... to be honest...

They were not 'making love.'

I blushed and crossed myself guiltily as I said the words silently in my head:

*They're fucking.*

Oh *God,* were they fucking.

Cat was pressed against the wall, her dress hiked up around her waist.

Valentino stood in front of her.

His pants were pulled down slightly below his ass, and Cat's legs were clamped around his waist.

His shirt covered his upper body, but his ass – his bare, beautiful, perfect ass – thrust back and forth, driving himself forward between Cat's open legs.

There was a wet slapping sound of skin on skin...

And Cat clawed at his back with her nails.

I could see her face over his shoulder.

Her eyes were closed, and her expression was caught somewhere between pain and ecstasy.

I don't think she was frowning because of actual pain –

But because she was trying to hold back the screams of pleasure every time Valentino thrust deep inside her.

Every time his beautiful ass rocked forward, her entire body jolted –

And a tiny, high-pitched *uh – uh – uh – UH* escaped her throat.

Sometimes she bit his shoulder or his neck to stop herself from screaming.

And his hands... his big, strong hands... grabbed at her ass, holding her up in the air effortlessly like a doll, as he had his way with her.

I stood there in absolute shock.

I knew how sex worked –

But I had never seen it.

Not videos on the internet, nor watching anyone do it before.

And it was the most beautiful – the most arousing – the most astounding thing I had ever seen in my life.

I was wetter than ever before...

Even more turned on than last night when Dario kissed me...

Even more than my dreams of him ravishing me.

All I could do was stand there, hypnotized, and watch as Valentino fucked her like a beast.

Suddenly Cat's cries began to increase in pitch and urgency –

And she pressed her face into his shoulder and gave one long, muffled scream.

"Oh fuck – oh *fuck* – oh FUCK – " Valentino grunted into her hair.

Suddenly he thrust *hard* and *deep* inside her –

And both of them held onto each other like they were dying.

Finally he pulled his face away from her hair and they began to kiss... tenderly, passionately...

But he still held onto her, her bare ass cupped in his huge hands...

His body still pressing against her.

I couldn't watch anymore.

I was going crazy from lust, and I couldn't bear it.

All I could think of was wanting to be in Cat's place...

But with Dario pressing me against the wall and *his* bare ass thrusting his manhood inside me.

I stumbled away from the door and out of the kitchen –

Right into the path of Filomena.

"Oh!" she exclaimed as I staggered into the hallway. "Are you alright, child?"

I stared at her like she was an alien.

I knew I couldn't let her go in the kitchen – I couldn't let Cat get caught –

But I had to do something about the overwhelming lust in my body –

The shame that I had watched a terrible sin.

Even worse, that I wanted to do it myself.

"I need to go to church," I mumbled. "I need to go to confession."

She smiled and nodded primly. "Good. I can ask one of the drivers to take you. There is a village close by – "

"No," I interrupted.

She looked surprised. "Why not?"

I winched. "Dario won't let me off the estate."

She scowled. "Of course not... why would a murderer allow an innocent to do that which God commands?"

I realized I had an ally, and I grabbed her hands as I beseeched her. "Is there another way off the grounds? A way to get to the church?"

Filomena looked around her as though afraid someone might hear her. Then she turned back to me and nodded. "Yes... but I can't take you there. I can *meet* you there, but I can't take you."

"What? Why?"

"Just trust me."

She told me to go to the west wing, past the chapel, and to a doorway at the far end of the corridor. I would know it because there was a *fleur-de-lis* – a lily of the field emblem – carved into the wood.

Once I got there, I was to knock. If there was no answer, I was to wait a minute and knock again, then keep knocking every 60 seconds until I got an answer.

"Go," she whispered. "I'll see you there."

I did as she said and walked down the hallway, unsure why she had sent me off alone.

When I found the door, I knocked once. No answer.

I counted to 60 and knocked again –

And this time, the door swung open.

I entered the room to find a small, cramped hallway. Filomena was there and beckoned me inside.

After I entered, she quickly shut the door behind me.

"This is part of the servants' passageways," Filomena explained. "They were used for centuries so servants could come and go without bothering the masters of the house. I was shown them when I began work here, but they also told me there is a way off the property if we were ever attacked."

I didn't have to ask who might attack the estate because I already knew:

Other *mafiosos.*

"Why couldn't you bring me here yourself?" I asked.

"Because the Rosolinis have eyes *everywhere...* and they'd *kill* me if they knew I brought you here."

I wanted to protest that they wouldn't... but the words died in my throat. I feared she was right.

Filomena led me down the small corridor to another door and opened it. There was nothing but yawning black until she hit a light switch. Suddenly, dozens of light bulbs spaced every 20 feet lit up a stone passageway stretching off into infinity.

"Follow the passageway," Filomena said. "It ends with an iron door that locks from the inside. Once closed, it will not open again. You will find yourself in a field. Go straight ahead through the forest, and you will eventually reach a wall. Travel left along the wall until you find a break in the stones, and you'll see a small town on the other side. There is a church in the town where you can say confession."

Suddenly she grasped my hands.

"My child... I beg you, take this opportunity to escape. This is a house of murder and sin... leave it and never come back."

"What about you?" I asked. "What will they do when they find out I'm gone?"

"They'll never suspect me," she said. "Don't worry, I'll be fine."

"Why don't you come with me?"

She smiled sadly and shook her head. "I'm an old woman. There is no place for me out there. I would die in misery. But you – *you* still have a chance. Go, before they realize you are gone."

"Thank you," I whispered.

She kissed my forehead. "May God bless you."

Then she turned back and closed the door behind me.

I stood there for a moment, overwhelmed by fear –

And then joy exploded through my body.

I was free!

I ran down the stone passageway as fast as I could, guided by the dim lightbulbs strung along the ceiling.

I finally reached the end of the corridor and found the iron door she had mentioned.

It took all my strength to turn the handle. It shrieked – but the door opened.

Stone steps led up to a dense canopy of underbrush. Daylight peeked through tiny gaps in the vines.

I held the heavy door open and remembered Filomena's words:

*Once closed, it will not open again.*

Once I let go of the door, my choice was final.

Fear raced through me –

But I thought of Dario in the chapel and what he had said:

*I will do whatever else I LIKE with you... and TO you. I will make you my whore... and when the time comes, you will beg me to take you.*

I thought of what I had seen in the pantry – Cat and Valentino coupling in the shadows –

And though I wanted it, I knew my soul was in danger.

If I stayed, I knew Dario would pursue me...

And I knew that I would eventually give in.

I let go of the door.

It swung closed behind me and latched with a metallic *CLANK.*

I tried the handle to be sure –

Locked.

The die was cast. There was no way but forward.

I fought through the vines and shrubs into the daylight, and left the Rosolinis – and Dario – behind...

...forever.

# 15

As I left the thicket of vines, I looked back over my shoulder. The western wing of the mansion was 200 feet behind me, and the house stretched far beyond that to the east. I turned and ran.

It was just as Filomena had said: a field, then a patch of forest.

I stumbled through the trees until I reached a stone wall at least 10 feet high.

There was no way I could get over it – and then I remembered what she had told me:

*Go left.*

I did as she said until I found a break in the stones: a huge gap like an earthquake had cracked the wall apart.

The breach was easy enough to squeeze through, and I found myself on a hill overlooking a tiny village.

Careful of snakes like the one I had encountered the other day, I made my way down the barren hillside until I reached the deserted cobblestone streets of the village.

It was an old place – and far smaller than Mensano, which only had 200 inhabitants.

If I had to guess, I would say fewer than 50 people lived here. It was a dying village populated by old folks who refused to leave their homes.

There were only a handful of stone buildings, but one of them was a church. It towered above me, a relic from centuries past.

I looked all around, but there was no one to be seen in the streets...

So I opened the wooden door of the church and went inside.

The interior was rustic, with a giant vaulted ceiling. Unlike the chapel in the mansion, it felt cold and impersonal. There was no art adorning the walls here – only bare stone.

"Hello?" I called out timidly.

Dozens of wooden pews surrounded me on all sides, and I slowly walked down the center aisle. Everything was quiet around me.

"Hello?" I said, louder this time. "Is anyone there?"

"Yes?" a man's voice answered from the rear of the church, startling me.

A priest in a black robe appeared out of the gloom. His face was thin with hollow cheeks, his wispy grey hair unkempt. He walked with a cane, and he looked up into the air as though searching the rafters for something.

I realized he was blind.

"Is someone there?" he called out.

I quickly moved closer to him. "I need your help."

His blank eyes gravitated towards my voice as he smiled. "Yes, my child?"

I felt uneasy. There was something unsettling about the way his eyes roved over me.

But he was a priest. I was finally safe.

"I need to call my father," I said. "He lives near Mensano."

"You're quite a ways from home. What are you doing here? Did your car break down?"

"No – the Rosolinis were holding me prisoner. I just now escaped."

"The Rosolinis!" he exclaimed, and his face suddenly darkened.

"Yes."

"And you escaped, you say?"

"Yes."

"Are you alright?"

"Yes, Father."

"They did not take advantage of you?"

"No."

"They did not... *sully* you?"

The way he said it was disturbing...

Like he was imagining me being touched – or worse –

And he almost seemed to enjoy it.

"No, they didn't do anything," I said with a frown. "But I need to call my father to let him know I'm alright."

"I'm afraid I don't have a telephone, my dear."

"None?" I asked in astonishment.

He held out his arms and gestured to the church around him. "As you can see, there is not much here. This is an old village and an even older church."

My heart filled with despair. "Well, someone in the village must have a phone, yes?"

"Probably, but – you escaped from the Rosolinis, you said?"

"Yes. Is there someone I could ask for in the village, someone with a phone?"

"How did you escape?"

"There was a passageway out the back," I said hurriedly. "I really need to contact my father – thank you, but I should go."

I turned to leave –

"Wait," he said. "I forgot – I have a cell phone. For emergencies."

I frowned. "I thought you didn't have a phone?"

"I use it so seldom," he said with a smile as he peered up sightlessly into the sky. "It slipped my mind. Come – come, I can let you use it."

He began to *tap tap tap* his cane towards the back of the church.

"Come – come, my child. Come with me."

I was afraid... but I followed him as he made his way into the shadows.

# 16

There was a room in the back of the church. Not exactly living quarters, but it contained a table and cabinets. The rest of the space was taken up with storage.

The priest closed the door to the church behind us. I noticed another smaller door, presumably an exit, off to my right.

"Sit, sit," he said as he felt his way along the cabinets lining the walls. "I'm sure my phone is here somewhere – I just have to find it."

I sat in one of the chairs and tried to suppress my rising panic.

I only had a limited amount of time before Dario and the others discovered I was gone. It might be hours... or it could be 30 minutes.

What would happen when they realized I was no longer on the grounds?

Would they figure out where I had gone?

"You said you escaped from the Rosolinis?" the old man asked as his hands rummaged through open drawers.

"Yes."

"You said they were holding you prisoner?"

"Yes."

"Why, exactly?"

"I... there was a murder in my father's café. I saw who did it."

The priest whirled around. "My child! Are you alright?"

"Yes, Father."

"That's so horrible... I am so sorry you had to witness that..."

"Thank you, Father."

He walked over to the table, sat down, and reached out for my hands. "Give me your hand. Please."

I reluctantly put my hand in his.

His skin felt leathery, his fingers bony.

"I'm glad you're alright," he said as he patted my skin.

"Can you find the phone, please?" I asked, trying to hurry him up. "I really need to call my father."

"Of course, of course," he said soothingly as his eyes roved along the ceiling. "I just want you to know that you're safe here."

"Thank you," I said, not convinced at all.

"How did you say you escaped?"

"There was a passageway."

"And where was it, exactly?"

I frowned. "What does it matter?"

A sound came from behind the door to the church.

I whirled around.

The door was still closed.

"Is there someone else here?" I asked, frightened.

"No, of course not," the priest said. "This is a very old building... it makes sounds sometimes."

I stared at the door... but I heard nothing else.

"I need to call my father," I repeated.

"Of course, of course," he said soothingly. "I'll get up and find the phone in a moment. I just wanted to make sure you're alright. The Rosolinis are monsters – I'm sure it was terrifying being held there against your will."

"It's fine. Nothing happened."

"Of course, of course. You're safe now. That's all that matters."

He still held my hand in his, which felt creepy... but I couldn't very well yank it away from him.

Suddenly there was another sound behind the door, like shoes scuffing on stone.

"Father, are you sure there's no one else here?!" I asked in a panic.

"I promise you, my child, we are alone."

I listened intently –

But I heard nothing else.

The priest chuckled. "If anyone could hear an intruder, it would be me – would you not agree?"

I looked at his blind eyes searching the air above me. "I guess..."

"Now, the passageway you mentioned – the one from the Rosolini's mansion – "

"Why do you care?!" I exclaimed, then desperately cried out, "I need to call my father! If you'll just tell me where the phone is, I'll find it on my own!"

I tried to pull my hand away –

But the priest held me tightly by the wrist.

I stared at him in horror –

Then struggled to pull away.

He held me even tighter, his hands like a vise.

"You must tell me how you escaped," he hissed. "If there is a passageway into the house – "

"Let go of me!" I cried out.

Suddenly I heard another sound behind the door, like it was creaking open –

And my terror gave me the strength to break away from the priest.

"STOP!" he yelled as I stumbled for the small door on the opposite side of the room.

I ignored him and exploded through the door into the daylight.

I looked around wildly.

I was in an alleyway between a stone wall and the church.

To my left was a dead end.

The street was 60 feet away to my right.

I started to run –

When the door burst open behind me, and a heavy body tackled me to the cobblestones.

I tried to scream, but a hand that stank of nicotine closed over my mouth.

"Quiet," a man's voice hissed in my ear, "or I'll gut you like a fish."

Strong hands flipped me roughly onto my back, and I found myself staring up at a stranger with brown hair and a scraggly beard. He wore a cheap suit and he smelled of cigarette smoke and sweat.

I heard the priest behind him. "Did you get her?"

"Yes," the stranger snarled. "Now get back inside."

The priest immediately slammed the door shut, leaving me at the mercy of my attacker.

The stranger turned back to me, malice in his eyes. "Now, you and I are going to have a little talk – "

That was when I bit down on his hand.

The taste of smoke and dirt was disgusting – but not as bad as the copper taste of blood.

"AAAAH!" he screamed, then slapped me. "You BITCH – you'll PAY for that!"

He pressed my face to the cobblestones with one hand, and I heard him fumble with his belt with the other. There was the metallic clink of his buckle and the sound of the leather strap.

"NO!" I screamed.

He cackled. "You're going to pay me back for what you – "

He was interrupted by the growl of a powerful engine – far away at first, then rapidly getting closer.

The man froze on top of me and listened as the engine roared ever louder.

Tires squealed in the street, a car door opened –

And Dario's voice yelled, "ALESSANDRA!"

The stranger tried to cover my mouth, but I jerked my head free and screamed, "DARIO!"

The stranger slapped me in retribution, then stumbled to his feet.

I looked over. Dario was running down the alleyway towards us, murder in his eyes.

The stranger reached inside his suit jacket and pulled something out.

At first I was afraid it was a gun –

And then I heard the *click!* of a switchblade opening.

Dario stopped abruptly.

The man lunged at him –

Dario jumped back –

And then the man swiped again.

Dario caught the stranger's arm and brought his knee up against the man's elbow, breaking it backwards with a *CRACK*.

"AAAAAH!" the stranger screamed as he fell to his knees.

Dario pried the knife from the man's hand, let it clatter to the cobblestones, and kicked it away.

Then he went absolutely insane.

He slammed his fist into the man's face –

Again –

And again –

And again.

Blood spattered across the stones –

And still Dario pummeled the stranger's face.

Finally he stopped and let the man fall limply to the ground.

When he finally turned towards me, Dario looked like a demon. His face was the personification of murder.

I thought for sure he would kill me in his fury.

As he reached down to me, I scrabbled backwards in the dirt –

But all he said was, "Are you alright?"

I stopped, trembling, and nodded *yes.*

"He didn't hurt you?" Dario asked.

I shook my head *no.* "He tried, but... you got here in time."

Dario's expression got even darker, if that was possible.

He turned back towards the stranger. I thought for a second that he was going to tear the man limb from limb –

When another engine roared up to the church.

Tires screeched, doors opened, and Adriano and Massimo ran into the alleyway.

"What the hell happened?!" Adriano shouted.

"Search the church!" Dario yelled, then turned to me. "Was there anyone else?"

"A p-priest," I stuttered.

"You heard her – GO!" Dario raged.

Adriano ran for the front of the church. Massimo opened the door I had come out of and disappeared inside.

Dario knelt beside me and put his powerful hands on my shoulders.

I thought he might shake me or strike me –

But all he did was stare into my eyes.

"...are you sure you're alright?" he asked, his voice quiet.

I tried to nod *yes* –

But my eyes welled up and I burst into tears.

He got down on the ground next to me and cradled me in his arms.

"Shhh... it's over... you're safe," he whispered in my ear. "You're safe."

He held me until my sobs subsided – and then I heard shouting from the front of the church.

"Get your hands off me!" howled a familiar old man's voice.

"Come on," Dario said as he lifted me effortlessly to my feet.

He put his arm around me and supported me as we walked to the front of the church.

A black Mercedes idled in the deserted street beside the midnight blue Bugatti.

The priest was kneeling on the ground in front of the cars.

Massimo stood behind him; one massive paw on the old man's shoulder forced him to stay on his knees.

A few feet away, Adriano paced back and forth like an enraged panther, a pistol in his hand.

When Dario and I emerged from the alleyway, Adriano gestured with his pistol at the priest. "This *stronzo* acts like he doesn't know what's going on."

"Leave me alone!" the old man cried out.

Dario nodded to Adriano, who pressed the barrel of the gun against the old man's forehead.

"Time to answer a few questions, *padre,*" Adriano snarled.

"Wait – stop – there's no reason for this," the priest said in a panicked voice.

"Who do you work for?" Dario asked.

The priest's blind eyes tracked the sound of Dario's voice. "The Church – I work for the Church! The pope, Rome, the Vatican!"

"I mean whoever *else* is lining your pockets."

"I didn't *do* anything! You have to believe me!"

Dario looked at me. "What happened?"

"He knew the man who attacked me," I said. "The priest *obeyed* him."

As soon as he heard my voice, the old man's expression went from frightened to resigned.

"Damn it... I thought maybe he'd gotten away with her." Then the priest smirked. "I guess not."

I stared at him in astonishment.

He had been faking his fear. It had all been a lie.

Adriano seemed stunned, too. "Who the hell *is* this bastard?!"

"Probably not even a priest," Dario said grimly. "Who's your accomplice, the one I nearly killed back there?"

"Ask him yourself, asshole," the old man croaked.

Adriano raised his gun and struck him across the face.

The old man yelped and went down on all fours.

Despite his evil intentions towards me, I still cried out in anguish.

After all, he was elderly – and a priest.

Or at least *dressed* like one.

But the next sound that came out of his mouth chilled me to the bone.

He began to laugh... a chuckle at first, then a rising cackle.

"Who are you, *really?*" Dario asked.

"Wouldn't you like to know."

"Fine. You'll talk plenty once we get you back to the house and Adriano goes to work on you."

"Damn straight," Adriano hissed.

"I don't think so, you – "

And the old man let out a string of vile curses that would have been shocking coming from a sailor, much less a priest.

Adrian pistol-whipped him again, opening up a cut across his cheek.

The old man snarled but didn't cry out this time.

"Careful, old man," Dario cautioned him, "or my brother will send you to your eternal reward."

"If that's the case, then I'll see you in *hell,* Dario Rosolini."

The old man sneered –

And suddenly began to froth at the mouth.

"What the – " Massimo exclaimed.

"Cyanide!" Dario roared.

He leapt over to the priest and shoved his finger into the man's jaws, trying to scoop out whatever poison was inside –

But it was too late.

The old man's body jerked a couple of times, and then he collapsed onto the ground. White foam continued to spill from his grinning mouth.

Dario suddenly looked like he'd realized something.

"The one in the alley!" he shouted at Massimo. "Go get him, NOW!"

Massimo turned and ran as fast as he could.

Meanwhile, Dario wiped his hand in disgust on the fake priest's robe.

"He's dead," Massimo's voice called out from the alleyway a few seconds later. "Same exact thing – cyanide."

Dario cursed, then yelled, "Does he have a wallet? A phone? Any identification?"

There was another pause, then Massimo said, "Nothing on him."

"What do you want to do?" Adriano asked Dario.

"Have Massimo put them in the trunk and haul them back to the house. I want *you* to search the church for any clue about who they work for. I'll send Valentino to help you."

"The priest said he had a cell phone in the back," I said, pointing to the rear of the church.

"Start there," Dario ordered his brother.

"Do we really want a bunch of dead bodies back at the house?" Massimo asked as he walked up.

"I don't want them lying around *here* while Adriano ransacks the place. It would be just our luck if the cops show up."

"We *own* the cops," Adriano said.

"Yes, and priests never commit suicide, either," Dario snapped. "Whoever paid these assholes might pay the police to fuck with us, too."

"Understood," Massimo said. He bent to pick up the priest as Adriano popped the Mercedes' trunk.

"Come on," Dario said as he took my hand.

"Where are we going?" I asked fearfully.

"Where do you think?" he snapped as he pulled me towards the Bugatti.

Once we were both inside the sports car, he started the engine and backed into the street.

"Dario – " I whispered.

"Don't," he snarled without looking at me.

"But – "

He turned and glared at me, his eyes furious.

"...thank you for saving me," I whispered.

He stared at me for a second longer, then turned back to the road.

Neither he nor I said another word on the way back to the mansion.

# 17

Dario

At first I felt only relief that Alessandra was safe.

Soon after that, I became furious with her for disobeying me –

But I put it aside.

There were more important things to worry about.

Two days ago, we had intercepted a spy in our territory. Lars had gunned him down at Alessandra's café, but we still didn't know what he was doing there in the first place.

Now I'd just found out there were *two* spies less than a mile away from my home –

And one of them had been deep undercover as a priest.

Spies who had killed themselves rather than subject themselves to questioning...

...probably because they knew it would have involved torture, and that we would have eventually broken them.

But they could have just *told* us. I would have let them live – even *paid* them – if they'd ratted out their employers.

But instead, they chose suicide over betrayal.

Who the hell amongst our enemies could command that kind of loyalty?!

I wasn't even certain the men in *our* organization would die for my family. Not like that.

The only ones I *was* sure about were my brothers and Lars.

Who was this phantom adversary who stalked our every move?

And what was his plan?

# 18

Alessandra

Niccolo, Lars, and Valentino were waiting for us as Dario's Bugatti drove into the garage.

"I spoke to Adriano on the phone," Niccolo said as soon as we got out of the sports car. "What the hell happened?!"

"Valentino, take her to the study," Dario ordered. He, Lars, and Niccolo stayed behind in the garage to talk.

The youngest Rosolini brother walked with me back to the house. He shook his head sympathetically. "I wouldn't want to be *you* for all the gold in the Vatican."

I spent ten long, agonizing minutes in the study, awaiting my fate –

But if I'd thought Dario was angry at me, it was *nothing* compared with Niccolo.

"What's WRONG with you?!" he roared as soon as he walked in.

"I didn't mean for anything to happen!" I cried out. "I only wanted to see a priest – "

"And you nearly got yourself killed! Do you understand now that we have enemies *everywhere?!* That these rules we give you are intended to keep you *safe?!*"

"I'm sorry!" I said as I held back my tears.

Niccolo spent the next several minutes asking questions about what had happened from the time I arrived in the church to when Dario had saved me.

I answered him truthfully every single time – until he asked, "What did you tell the priest?"

"Nothing!"

"Don't give me that!" he yelled. "The safety of everyone in this house depends on what you told him! What was it?!"

I tried to remember what I'd said to the blind man. "I told him I'd come from your house – that I was being held prisoner – that was it, I swear!"

"Did he ask *how* you escaped?"

"He did, but I didn't tell him any details."

"Speaking of which, how DID you get out?"

My mind raced through my options.

If I admitted to knowing about the secret exit, I would get Filomena in terrible trouble.

I remembered what she'd said:

*They'd KILL me if they knew I brought you here.*

I couldn't put her in that kind of danger... not when she'd only tried to help me.

Niccolo could see I was stalling.

"I want the TRUTH, not the best LIE you can come up with!" he bellowed.

I revealed as little as I could while I attempted to come up with a plausible explanation.

"...there's a crack in the wall surrounding your property," I said.

"We know that – it's been there forever. My grandfather escaped through it 50 years ago with my grandmother, father, and uncle when a rival family attacked the estate. My grandfather believed it was good luck and refused to patch it up, and my father followed his example. But how did *you* find it?"

He didn't mention anything about the secret exit from the mansion...

So I kept quiet, hoping he didn't know *that* was how I'd escaped.

"I... I just did," I said lamely.

"That's not good enough!"

"I've been trying to escape since the moment I got here! You didn't think I would *eventually* find it?" I snapped. I sounded much braver than I felt.

Niccolo looked at me suspiciously. "But how did you know about the church? How did you know where the town was?"

I was afraid that I might have to tell him the truth –

And then I remembered what had happened before I'd met Filomena in the hallway.

I'd been in the kitchen...

Where I'd seen Cat and Valentino having sex in the pantry...

But before that, I had done something else.

Something I'd forgotten until now.

"There was a cell phone I looked at," I said. "I searched for the nearest church on Google Maps and it told me which way to go."

"Who gave you their phone?!" Niccolo raged, and I realized I might have doomed Caterina by trying to save my own skin.

"No one! It was just lying there when I snuck into the kitchen," I said, trying to conceal Cat's identity.

"What, a cell phone was just *conveniently* sitting on the counter, unlocked and ready for you to use?"

"I think whoever it belonged to just stepped away for a moment. I saw the map, then I put it back where I found it. I swear it's the truth."

Niccolo glared at me. "I'll be checking your story."

I prayed that even if he questioned Caterina, Valentino would come to her aid.

"But in the meantime," Niccolo continued, "you had better make amends with someone else."

"...Dario," I said guiltily.

Just then, someone knocked lightly on the door.

"Come in," Niccolo barked.

A male servant came into the room. He carried a silver tray stacked with towels, bandages, tubes of ointment, and a bucket of ice.

"Give it to her and leave us," Niccolo commanded.

The servant handed me the tray, which I took in confusion. "What am I supposed to do with this?"

"Go to Dario and tend to his hand... which he injured saving YOU," Niccolo snapped.

My eyes grew wide. "I don't think that's such a good idea..."

"Oh, you don't, do you? Then perhaps you should reconsider disobeying him and fleeing the property – oh, wait! Too late for *that!*" Niccolo said mockingly. "Go to his private study on the third floor. Turn right at the top of the staircase, then it's two doors on your left. Make peace with him, *whatever* the price. Understood?"

I nodded... and wondered fearfully what that price might be.

As I was walking out, I stopped and turned back to Niccolo.

"Yes?" he asked testily.

"How did Dario know where I was?"

Niccolo looked at me like I was an idiot. "Are you forgetting your little temper tantrum last night? As soon as we discovered you were missing, we guessed you were headed for the nearest church. Thank god we were right."

"But... why did Adriano and Massimo show up, too?"

"As backup, of course!" Niccolo yelled. "What, you think we let the head of the family run around without protecting him?"

I frowned. Dario had shown up first, by almost a minute. If someone had been lying in wait to hurt him, Adriano and Massimo would have arrived too late.

"But – "

"GO!" Niccolo shouted, and I quickly scurried out of the room.

But as I left, I couldn't shake the feeling that he hadn't been entirely truthful.

# 19

I followed Niccolo's instructions and found a closed door down the hall. I knocked gently.

"Come in," Dario's muffled voice said.

I entered the room to see him glowering at me from behind an ornate desk. The shelves lining the walls were filled with leather-bound books and ancient marble busts.

"What do you want?" he snapped.

I held up the tray. Its contents rattled slightly in my trembling hands. "Niccolo said that... that I should come in and tend to your hand."

Dario narrowed his eyes. "Is that all?"

"...and to say thank you. Again. For saving me."

He stared at me angrily. "And?"

"...and to apologize. For running away."

"For disobeying me," he growled.

A couple of hours ago, those words – *For disobeying you* – would have stuck in my throat. If I'd said them at all, I would have spat them out from between clenched teeth.

But a lot had happened in the last two hours.

All I could smell was the stranger's nicotine-stained hand over my mouth...

And all I could hear was the *clink* of his belt buckle as he undid his pants.

"...for disobeying you," I whispered.

That seemed to satisfy Dario somewhat. He gestured with his head, and I walked over next to him.

There was an ottoman next to his chair. I sat down on it while I did my work.

I took his hand tenderly in mine and examined it. He had washed off the blood from my attacker, but the knuckles were bruised, scraped, and swollen.

I packed some ice in one of the towels, wet the cloth with melted water in the bucket, and put it on his hand.

He watched me angrily the entire time.

I looked up at him, then averted my eyes as I continued to apply the ice.

Finally he spoke. "Do you understand now why I didn't want you to leave the grounds? Why I refused your request to go to a church?"

"Yes," I murmured with downcast eyes.

"One of our enemies showed up at your café two nights ago. Now we've found spies just a mile from my house – and one of them was masquerading as a priest, no less. When I order you to do something, it's not just to protect the family, but to protect *you*. The people who want to kill us would gladly do the same to you just because you're staying here."

I wanted to say, *I think you mean 'just because you're IMPRISONED here'* –

But I decided now wasn't the time to speak my thoughts.

"I know," was all I murmured.

"More and more, I find the people around me are either my enemies or paid *off* by my enemies."

"Don't you have allies?" I asked.

"Not since my father died, it seems," he said bitterly.

Neither of us said anything else for a couple of minutes.

Finally I removed the wet towel, dried his hand, and began to dab a sweet-smelling ointment on his skin. Then I wrapped a bandage around his knuckles and his palm.

The process was slow and relaxing. Eventually my fear began to subside.

His hand was huge – it dwarfed mine. And his fingers were so calloused... so rough and manly...

When I finished, I put everything back on the tray. "I'll leave you now."

I got up to go and was halfway to the door when he spoke.

"Stop."

I turned slowly to look at him. My stomach was churning. "...yes?"

He smiled evilly. "You disobeyed me. Did you think you were going to escape unpunished?"

My heart skipped a beat.

"I'm sorry," I whispered. "I promise not to do it again."

He stood up behind the desk. "I don't care what you promise you'll do in the future; I only care what you've already *done*. Now came here."

I timidly walked back to the desk, afraid of what he might do.

"Take off your panties," he commanded.

I stared at him. "W-what?"

"You heard me."

"I..."

I came up with the stupidest excuse possible.

"...I can't. My hands are full."

"Put it down."

I swallowed hard, then put the tray on top of the desk.

"Now do it," he ordered.

"I... please, don't," I said, my eyes welling up.

He rounded the desk and snarled, "I don't want your tears – I want you to *obey me*. Now take off your panties."

I steeled myself as I imagined the most terrible things he was about to do to me.

I slowly bent down to the hem of my dress...

...pulled it up on both sides so at least my front was covered...

...and slowly pulled off my underwear and let it drop around my ankles.

Then I let go of my dress and let it fall down to my knees again.

I couldn't look at him as I did it. My face was blushing bright red, and my entire body trembled in fear.

"Step out of them," he said, his voice husky. He no longer sounded angry.

I glanced up at him.

There was something else in his face now as he stared at me:

Desire.

I began to breathe harder, my chest rising and falling, as I slowly stepped away and left my undergarments on the floor.

I thought of our kiss the night before, and suddenly I felt a growing heat between my legs.

But I didn't think tonight would end with only a kiss.

Which both thrilled me...

And terrified me.

He walked over and got right up next to me.

"Pull your dress up to your thighs," he commanded in a low voice. "And look at me while you do it."

I stared into his dark, terrible eyes as I bent over and slowly pulled up my dress to my thighs.

His hand reached down and grabbed the hem of my dress.

"Please – " I said, frightened –

"Be quiet," he said, his voice a low growl.

I closed my mouth, though my lips quivered with fear.

He watched me, and I stared at him...

And I felt his fingertips graze the inside of my thighs, light as a feather.

"Oh," I half-gasped, half-whispered.

"Has anyone ever touched you here before?"

My mouth was dry, and I could not speak. All I could do was shake my head *no*.

"So I'm the first," he murmured.

His fingers slowly traced their way up the inside of my leg.

I whimpered in fear and shame.

The fear was understandable.

The shame came from letting a man do this to me –

Of letting *il Mostro* do this to me –

And me wanting him to do more.

His fingers got all the way to the top of my legs... and then paused.

I stared into his dark eyes and felt like I was drowning.

I wanted to scream *Stop!* –

...but another voice inside me whispered, *Keep going... PLEASE keep going...*

It was the whisper that he listened to.

His finger touched the hairs on my sex, tickling me, stroking me –

And then suddenly the tip of his finger found wet, bare skin.

I gasped.

He glided slowly along my lips until he reached the top...

Where his finger found a swollen pearl of desire.

He began to slowly circle it...

The gentlest of touches...

And I began to moan.

I had never felt *anything* like this before.

No one had ever touched me there –

And I had *certainly* never done anything like this myself.

It was sinful pleasure –

Lust and desire and all the things I had been warned about forever –

And I *loved* it.

But I tried to resist...

I truly did.

"Stop," I whispered as his fingertip slowly caressed me down there.

"No," he growled softly into my ear.

He began to circle me with slightly more pressure...

And the pleasure inside me doubled.

"Oh please... stop," I moaned.

His lips brushed against my ear. I shivered as he whispered, "No."

His finger began to stroke up and down.

The little button of pleasure between my legs grew hotter and hotter. I felt an incredible need, a terrible urge for something to fill me up – for something to come inside me, deep inside me –

"Please stop!" I sobbed – not with tears, but overwhelmed with pleasure and emotion and feelings I had never even imagined.

"No," he said in a guttural growl.

His other hand reached up to the front of my dress and found my right nipple, hard and stiff beneath my bra... and he began to stroke it, too.

Between my legs, his finger began to rub faster – harder –

As his other fingers lightly pinched my nipple –

And it felt like my legs might give way beneath me.

I grabbed onto his muscular arms and held on for dear life.

The most pleasurable heat imaginable rolled through me like a wave from my thighs up into my body.

My eyelids fluttered and closed involuntarily – I could no longer keep them open.

"OH GOD!" I cried out as pleasure filled my entire body.

Waves of ecstasy took hold of me. Muscles I didn't know I had fluttered in my belly.

My legs gave way beneath me, and my ass collapsed back against the desk.

Suddenly his mouth was on mine, his lips pressing hard against mine.

I kissed him desperately as the heat and pleasure inside me reached a crescendo.

My fingers dug into his arms as I pulled away from his kiss and screamed like I was dying.

A few seconds later, his finger began to slow down...

And the pressure began to ease off as he gently circled the tiny pearl of desire between my legs.

Still, wave after wave of pleasure rolled through my body.

Not as powerful... not as intense... more like water lapping on the beach after a giant wave has crashed on the sand.

Finally it was over... but I stayed there, my eyes closed, not wanting it to end.

I felt his hands move away from my thighs and my breast.

Seconds later, Dario pulled me upright and set me on my feet.

My eyes fluttered open and I stood there in a daze.

Dario was staring at me. He looked insane...

Or consumed with maddening hunger...

Like a starving wolf just seconds away from devouring a fawn.

"Get out," he said hoarsely.

I stared at him, confused. "...what?"

"That was your punishment. Now *get out.*"

I frowned. "But – "

He leaned down in my face and said angrily, "*Get... OUT.*"

I stumbled away from him, suddenly ashamed of what had just happened...

Ashamed of the wetness slicking the inside of my thighs...

Ashamed that I wanted *more.*

I knelt to grab my underwear from the ground –

"Leave them and GET OUT!" he thundered.

I stumbled out of the room, tears flowing down my face.

I hurried back to my room, where I collapsed on my bed and wept...

...both for my lost innocence...

...and at his bewildering cruelty.

# 20

Dario

I nearly lost control.

If she had stayed there an instant longer, I might have.

The feel of her breast beneath my hand – her nipple between my finger and thumb –

Her wetness as I circled her clit –

The way she screamed when she came –

I felt like an animal.

My cock was hard as steel beneath my pants. She made me so hard it *hurt*.

I wanted to throw her down on the desk, ravage her, thrust deep inside her and fuck her like a raging bull –

But she was a virgin.

It would have hurt her – turned all her pleasure to pain –

And I had made a promise.

I wouldn't take her until she begged.

So I had to make her leave before I gave in to my animal desires.

She'd stared at me with wounded eyes as I yelled at her to leave – but finally she did.

I leaned against the desk, panting with desire, still smelling her scent in the air long after she fled.

I lifted my finger, the one I had touched her clit with, and tasted her.

She was both sweet and musky... like watermelon and a hint of cloves...

And I knew that the next time I 'punished' her, I would have to taste her for real.

# 21

Alessandra

That evening, Filomena brought my dinner up to me on a tray. While setting out the food, she gently informed me that Niccolo said I was confined to my room until further notice.

That was probably for the best. I had no idea how I could ever face Dario again after what he had done to me – much less see him in front of all his brothers.

After I ate, I grew groggy and fell into a deep and dreamless sleep.

When I woke up the next morning, all the physical tension in my body was gone. I felt *so* relaxed...

But I was sad as I lay there in the early morning light.

All I could think about was Dario...

His hands touching me...

Giving me so much pleasure...

And then him acting like Dr. Jekyll and Mr. Hyde and forcing me out of the room.

I also felt horrible for another reason.

No one had ever done *anything* like that to me before.

I knew it was wrong...

To be touched like that before marriage...

To be with a man out of wedlock...

But I had *loved it.*

And I felt shame that I wanted more.

I tried to resist, but what Dario had made me feel was too powerful.

I worked up my courage as I lay there in bed...

Pulled up my negligee...

And hesitantly touched between my legs.

I'd never done it before, and it felt awkward and unsatisfying.

I tried to mimic Dario's actions... but even when I found the spot that had felt so good yesterday, it still wasn't *nearly* as good as what *he* had done.

What I *wanted* was for HIM to touch me.

I closed my eyes...

And imagined his smell – that expensive cologne he wore...

The mesmerizing depths of his dark eyes...

His muscles...

And as I touched myself and thought of him, my pleasure increased within seconds.

I imagined it was *his* finger down there caressing me.

Tiny waves of pleasure rippled through my belly...

But it *still* wasn't as good as him...

And I gave up trying.

Not only that, I was ashamed I'd done something I wasn't supposed to.

*Although,* I thought wryly, *I don't think I'll be going to confession anytime soon.*

After I showered and dressed, I went down to the kitchen.

As soon as Cat saw me, she turned away in silence.

*Oh no...*

I winced as I asked, "Did Niccolo talk to you?"

Cat looked at me with both anger and fear. "You could have gotten me killed – you *know* that, right?!"

"I didn't tell him it was you!" I protested frantically. "I just said I found a phone and looked at it – "

"And then you ran off and disobeyed Don Rosolini!" she hissed. "Niccolo threatened to fire me! I could have lost *everything!*"

"I just figured that Valentino would have stepped in and protected you," I mumbled.

Cat looked wary. "And why would he have done *that?*"

"Well... because... you know."

Cat looked a little afraid. "No, I don't."

I tilted my head to the side in exasperation. "I saw you in the pantry yesterday."

Cat's eyes nearly bugged out of her head – and then she buried her face in her hands. "Oh my God... oh my God, oh my God, oh my God..."

"I didn't tell Niccolo," I whispered.

Cat pulled her head out of her hands and looked up at the ceiling.

"I *told* him we couldn't do it in here... I *told* him we would get caught..." Then she looked at me angrily. "And YOU – you little pervert, spying on us!"

I flushed bright red. "I'm – I'm sorry..."

Cat scowled at me –

Then the corner of her mouth twitched the tiniest bit...

And she burst out laughing.

"Sainted Virgin, your face!... I'm just kidding with you. I mean, I'm not exactly *happy* you watched us – but let's just say I'm glad it was *you* and not somebody else." Cat smiled impishly. "To be honest, I totally would've watched, too."

I still felt absolutely mortified and couldn't speak.

She giggled and patted my hand.

"It's fine, it's fine," she said, then looked at me like I was a naughty child. "I'm still pissed about the phone, though."

"I'll do whatever I can to make it up to you," I promised.

"Hmph," she said playfully, then broke out into an excited smile. "He's *amazing,* isn't he?"

All I could do was imagine myself in the pantry, pressed against the wall, with Dario inside me.

I was suddenly *very* hot and wet, and I pressed my legs together uncomfortably.

Cat didn't notice. She was still imagining yesterday as she bit her lower lip and rolled her eyes.

"Oh my god... the way he makes me feel... it's like no other man I've ever been with." Then she looked at me, her eyes sparkling. "Who's the best you've ever been with?"

"I... I haven't," I stammered.

She stared at me like I had three eyes. "You've *never* had *sex* before?!"

"...no..."

"Oh my god, you poor girl... we have to get you laid." She playfully pointed at me. "Not Valentino, though – he's *mine.*"

I frantically shook my head *no.* "I would never – "

"Have you ever even *kissed* anyone?" she interrupted.

"I... y-yes..."

Her face shone with excitement. "How far did you let him go?"

I swallowed and thought of Dario's hand beneath my dress.

"I... he touched me..."

Cat waited expectantly.

"...down there," I whispered, pointing below my waist.

I couldn't believe I was sharing this private information with a woman who was basically a stranger –

But I figured I owed her for the trouble I'd gotten her into.

...plus it turned me on to actually talk about it.

"You let him finger you?!" Cat squealed.

"I... I guess...?"

She frowned. "What's the matter with you? Don't you know what he did?"

I shrugged like, *Sort of...?*

"Oh my god, you really *are* a good little Catholic girl, aren't you?" Cat said, realizing how inexperienced I was. She immediately leaned over the counter to gossip. "All right, tell me *exactly* what he did to you."

"He... he took his finger and... he touched this spot that felt really good..."

"Ohhhhh... he stroked your clit," she said knowingly. "Not bad. Before Valentino, I was lucky if a guy even knew I *had* one, much less find it."

"...my clit?" I asked. I had no idea what she was talking about.

"Your clitoris," Cat said casually.

When I didn't reply, she said, *"Madonn...* didn't *anybody* explain the birds and bees to you?"

I frowned in annoyance. "I know about sex."

And I did. My mother had explained how babies were made and how I would get my period.

But she died when I was 12. After that, my father never spoke of sex – and I had no aunts or grandmother to tell me more.

"Explain it to me, then," Cat demanded.

"When a husband and wife love each other very much – "

"Man and *woman,*" she interrupted. "And they don't exactly have to *love* each other – trust me. My God, the Church has brainwashed you... do you even *know* what your clit is?"

I feel absolutely mortified that I was so ignorant and shook my head *no.*

Cat sighed heavily. "Let me draw you a picture – no, wait, this is better."

There was a bowl of freshly made dough nearby. Cat pulled out a huge handful, slapped it down on the countertop, and began shaping it.

"Alright, these are your legs... see? And this is your pussy."

I blushed to hear her say the word, but I watched with intense interest.

"The pussy is the whole thing, but it has different parts. You have the vagina, which is the hole that the guy sticks his cock in. Once you're nice and wet, that is. Around the vagina are the labia, the lips. You have outside lips and inside lips... and if you follow them all the way up to the top, that's where you find your clit."

She made a pea-sized ball of dough and put it at the top of the slit. Then she crimped a little bit more dough and made a sort of half-blanket over the tiny sphere.

"There's also a hood over the clit, and that feels really good, too – but it's the clit that's the most sensitive. For some women, it's *too* sensitive – and for *most* women, you have to warm her up first before touching her clit directly. But once you do, it's *fantastic.*" Cat slowly moved her fingertip around the pea in a circle. "Is that what he did to you?"

I hadn't *seen* it, obviously, but what she was doing seemed remarkably similar to what Dario had done.

I nodded vigorously, my cheeks blazing hot –

And my...

*(Oh God, I can't even say it)*

...my pussy got even wetter.

Cat grinned. "How did it feel?"

"AMAZING," I blurted out, then blushed even harder.

She laughed out loud. "What happened?!"

"He just keep touching it... circling it... stroking it..."

"Stop, you're getting *me* turned on," Cat laughed as she fanned herself with one hand. "Did he make you come?"

I stared at her. "What's that?"

Cat's head fell forward on her neck like she couldn't believe I'd even said it. "You don't know what an *orgasm* is?!"

"I've *heard* of it..."

"Oh my God, were you raised in a *nunnery?*" She didn't wait for me to answer. "It's this amazing feeling through your pussy and parts of your body. It's, like, this intense pleasure – "

"Like you're sneezing down there, and it feels really good, and you do it over and over and over again?" I asked.

Cat laughed. "Oh shit, it sounds like you came!"

My cheeks burned bright red again.

*Dario made me come...*

"Daaaamn... you're practically a nun, and the first guy who touched you gave you an orgasm? Lucky girl," Cat purred. Then she asked excitedly, "Who was he?"

*A mafioso.*

*The man who runs this entire estate and crime family.*

"...just a guy..." I said quietly.

"Wow... well, if he could get you off the first time with his fingers, imagine what he could do with his cock."

I felt like I was burning up.

Both my face –

*And* my pussy.

Cat groaned. "Now *I'm* all turned on! I am *not* fucking Valentino in the pantry again, so no more sex talk!"

That was fine by me.

All I could think of was Dario touching me...

Touching my clit...

And making me come, over and over –

"Alright," Cat said, interrupting my daydream, "want to make it up to me for screwing me over with Niccolo?"

"Yes, of course," I said, grateful for something else to think about.

"Good." She pointed at a nearby counter where there was a beautiful wooden tray and a plate filled with fruit, fresh bread, and butter. "Once I make a cup of espresso, I need you to take that up to Don Rosolini."

My entire body jerked as I stared at her. "...Dario?"

Cat looked over her shoulder with an amused expression.

"My, aren't *we* forward! Yes, the boss. He wants some breakfast before he works." She leaned forward and whispered, "He scares me a little."

*Tell me about it.*

I blushed even harder. "I... I don't think that's a good idea..."

She frowned as she worked the levers on an expensive coffee machine, and it began to hum and churn. "Why not?"

"He's..."

*He's the one who made me come.*

"...uh, he's very angry with me."

"I'll bet, after you ran off like that," she said as she filled a porcelain cup with dark, steaming coffee. "Well, here's your chance to make it up to him *and* me."

"Caterina..." I said in a pleading voice.

She frowned at me crossly as she set the cup down on the tray. "Oh, so you'll look at my phone and *watch me having sex* – THEN you'll get me in trouble and nearly get me fired! But when I ask you to help me with one little favor – *nooooooo.*"

I closed my eyes.

I felt awful.

And... to be truthful...

Part of me hoped that Dario would 'punish' me again.

"...alright," I whispered.

"Good!" Cat said gleefully and clapped her hands like a child. "Thank you."

I sighed heavily as I picked up the tray. "Where am I going?"

"His bedroom."

I stared at her. "His *bedroom?!*"

"That's where he wants it."

I winced. "Caterina – "

"Don't you dare back out now, you little pervert!"

I gasped. "Why did you call me that?!"

I thought it was because she knew what might happen if I went to his bedroom...

"Because you like watching people fuck," she said and snorted with laughter. "Use the internet from now on – it's *full* of porn."

I groaned inwardly. "Where's his bedroom?"

"Second floor on the east wing, all the way at the end."

Now I stared at her in terror. "Oh no..."

"What now?"

"The east wing is the *one* place Niccolo said I was to never go!"

She made a face. *"I* was supposed to go up there, so it's fine."

"No, Caterina, really, I can't – "

She put her hands on her hips and looked at me sternly. "Really? You steal my phone, run away from the house, watch me fuck in the pantry, nearly get me fired – but going down a *hallway* is too much for you?"

I groaned, closed my eyes... and turned around to walk out of the kitchen.

I was going to regret this. I just *knew* it.

"That's the spirit!" Cat called after me. "Try not to get me in trouble again on your way up there!"

## 22

I slowly carried the tray up the stairs. I was so nervous that the espresso cup rattled slightly in its saucer.

I got to the second floor... held my breath... and started walking down the hall to the left.

I just *knew* at any second that Niccolo was going to jump out of the shadows, point at me, and yell, "AHA!"

The closer I got to the end of the eastern wing, the harder my heart thudded in my chest.

When I finally reached the closed door at the end of the hallway, I rapped on it lightly.

"H-hello?"

No answer.

I knocked a little harder.

"...hello?"

I looked behind me down the hall.

No one was there.

And Caterina said to deliver it to the room, so...

I turned the knob and the door opened.

I stood there in shock as I stared at a truly magnificent bedroom.

It was larger than any other room in the house except for the dining room.

There was a king-sized canopy bed to my left. Gauzy curtains hung down all around it, and the comforter was pulled back over rumpled sheets.

Masterpieces from Italian Renaissance painters hung on the walls.

Thick Arabian rugs covered the hardwood floors.

There were several mahogany wardrobes and a matching desk in the corner.

And a twenty-foot section of the wall had French doors that looked out on a massive balcony. Beyond that was a gorgeous view of the vineyards and orchards.

*My* bedroom was nice, but *this...* this looked like it belonged to a king.

I stood there staring at the opulence of it all...

And suddenly realized why Dario hadn't answered my knocking.

I could hear the *shhhhhh* of a shower from behind a half-closed door to my right.

I swallowed hard.

*Just put the tray down on the desk over there and walk out,* I told myself.

But another little voice – a tiny devil on my shoulder – whispered in my ear.

*You can look!*

*One tiny peek can't hurt...*

*You probably won't see anything, anyway.*

Once I set the tray on the desk, my feet carried me over to the door like a sleepwalker.

The shower was louder now as I peeked through the half-open door.

The room was beautiful, full of marble and gold –

But *that* wasn't what I looked at.

Halfway across the bathroom was a giant cube with walls of glass...

And Dario stood naked in the middle, his face held up to the spray of water.

My mouth dropped open.

He was absolutely gorgeous.

It was like looking at a Greek god.

Or an Italian one.

A god, anyway.

Albeit one with tattoos all over.

His shoulders were *so* broad... his chest so powerful...

His biceps were so big that they strained against his olive skin.

His body was all muscle. His stomach was ribbed like a washboard – a six-pack, I think the Americans call it.

And then my eyes dropped even further –

And I gasped.

I had seen a couple of penises in my life – boys swimming in the river near Mensano when I was a teenager. Theirs had been small.

Dario's was *not* small.

It dangled long and thick between his muscular thighs as water cascaded off it.

When he moved, it swung slowly. I could tell it would be heavy if I held it in my hand.

And at the thought of that –

Of me holding it in my hand –

Caressing it...

Stroking it...

Kissing it...

I nearly started hyperventilating.

Everywhere he'd touched me last night –

*My pussy,* I thought guiltily, still not used to the word –

Felt like it was on fire.

Pleasurable fire, but on fire nonetheless.

But how could it be on fire when I was suddenly so *wet?*

Suddenly Dario wiped the water from his eyes and turned towards me.

I freaked out.

I don't know if he saw me, but I turned and ran out of the bedroom as fast as I could.

I sped down the hallway, raced down the stairs, and made a beeline straight for the kitchen.

I wasn't thinking. All I knew was that I had to return to something normal, to something familiar – and Cat was the closest thing to normal and familiar that I had.

As soon as I walked in, she turned to me. "Ah, so you didn't die!"

I shook my head *no* as I sat on one of the stools by the central island.

"Did you see Don Rosolini?" she asked as she went back to cutting strawberries.

"...sort of," I said in a squeaky little voice.

Cat looked over at me with a frown. "What happened?"

"Nothing!" I said quickly.

She put down the knife. "Spill," she ordered.

I put my head in my hands, overcome with shame. "I... heard the shower in the bathroom..."

She gasped. "YOU WENT OVER THERE AND LOOKED?!"

Still hiding my face with my hands, I nodded.

"Oh my GOD, you *ARE* a little pervert!" she cackled. "If there's something you shouldn't look at, you just go right for it, don't you?"

Then she paused.

"Wait... *did you see Don Rosolini NAKED?*" she whispered.

I peeked one eye out from between my fingers... and nodded.

"OH MY GOD, OH MY GOD!" she shrieked.

"Shhhhh!" I said, trying to quiet her.

She raced over next to me and grabbed my hands. "What did he look like?" she whispered, her face only a few inches from mine.

My eyes closed involuntarily for a second. "Like a Greek god..."

"Unh!" she murmured, biting her lip. "Valentino's incredibly hot, but I mean... *Don Rosolini...* oh my god, I'm so jealous." She grinned and whispered, "Was he... big?"

I stared at her. "I... guess?"

"Oh, yeah, you wouldn't really know, would you?"

"How big is it normally?" I asked innocently.

"Ask any man and he'll tell you he's at *least* two inches bigger than he actually is. But I've seen a few in my time, so..."

She went back over to the bowl and pulled out a hunk of dough that she rolled into a tube maybe three inches long. "I'd say they're about *that* big when they're soft – and probably double that when they're hard."

I stared at her. "They get hard?"

She laughed. "Well, of course they do! Otherwise, how would you get it in your pussy? It'd be like trying to stick an overcooked piece of spaghetti in a hole."

I hadn't thought of that.

She grinned, reached out for the nearest fruit bowl, and seized a large banana. "Valentino's a *lot* bigger than your average guy. Yeah... that's about right," she said as she circled her fingers around the banana.

Then she looked at me gleefully. "So... how big was Don Rosolini?"

I raised an eyebrow at the banana, which was so firm that it didn't seem to be a good comparison.

"Hand me the bowl of dough," I said.

She pushed it over eagerly and watched as I scooped out a couple of handfuls and started rolling them into one long tube.

I paused... then added some more dough and rolled.

Then added a little bit more.

"Jesus!" Cat exclaimed. "What the hell, was he jerking off in the shower?"

"...what?"

She rolled her eyes. "Don't tell me you don't know about – never mind, of *course* you don't. Jerking off is when a guy is stroking his own dick," she said as she moved her hand through the air.

"Would it have been hard if he was... jerking off?"

She laughed. "Yes."

"Then he wasn't jerking off."

Cat stared at me –

Then looked down at the cylinder of dough in my hand.

"OH MY GOD!" she cried out, then began fanning herself with one hand.

"What?!"

"He's really hung!" she whispered. *"Madonn..."*

"Is that... good?" I asked, seriously bewildered.

"I wouldn't mind finding out!" Cat said with a snort.

For some reason, I felt a stab of jealousy when she said it.

*You already have Valentino,* I wanted to snap.

Suddenly there was a sharp knock behind me.

Both Cat and I jumped in fright.

I whirled around to see Valentino at the doorway, smirking. "What are you two talking about?"

The blood rushed to my cheeks. "NOTHING!"

"Nothing!" Cat yelped at the same time, though not as loud as me.

Valentino raised one eyebrow as he looked back and forth between me and Cat.

Then he glanced down at the counter in front of me.

I looked down to see what he was looking at –

And saw the long tube of dough.

I hastily pounded it with one fist and smashed it all together.

"Just making bread! Ha ha!" I said, forcing a laugh that made me sound crazy.

Valentino frowned at how strange I was acting, then jerked his head back towards the hallway. "Dario wants to see you."

I suddenly felt like I couldn't breathe.

I looked around at Cat in a panic –

And her hand flew up to her mouth in shock.

"W-w-why?" I stuttered.

"Who knows," Valentino said as he strolled past me and went over to Cat.

"Where is he?" I asked, then added hopefully, "His study?"

"No, his bedroom," he said as he took a piece of strawberry off the cutting board, threw it in the air, and caught it in his mouth.

I was nearly out of my mind with panic.

I looked over at Cat in desperation –

And her mouth dropped open in the biggest grin I've ever seen, like she was about to cheer.

She immediately went back to normal (to hide her excitement) when Valentino finished eating his strawberry.

*Then* she suddenly looked shocked.

She glared at Valentino like, *What the hell are you DOING?!*

I couldn't see because he was standing right next to her, but I would have bet money that his hand was on her ass.

He just ignored her like nothing unusual was going on.

"Well?" he asked as he looked at me.

"W-well what?"

Cat made a little *eep!* noise and grasped the edge of the counter.

I was betting Valentino's hand had traveled somewhere else...

But he *still* didn't let on that anything was amiss.

"Shouldn't you go?" he asked, pointing at the door with his free hand.

God only knows what he was doing to Cat with the other one.

"Uh... okay," I said with a tremulous voice.

I looked fearfully at Cat over my shoulder as I walked out of the kitchen.

She gave me a thumbs-up and smile like *You've got this!*

The last thing I heard as I closed the door was Cat giggling and gasping, "Oh!" –

And then the pantry door opened and quickly shut.

# 23

I stood outside his bedroom for almost 30 seconds before I found the courage to knock on the closed door.

More like gentle rapping, really.

Actually, just the faintest tap.

There wasn't any answer, so I turned to go –

"Come in," Dario's voice said from within.

I winced.

*Oh no...*

When I opened the door and walked in, I felt like I was wearing lead boots.

Then I gasped.

Dario was leaning over his desk, looking at something on a laptop.

He had on dark slacks –

But the rest of him was naked.

His skin was still damp from the shower. Droplets of water traced the curves of his muscles, and his wet hair hung in strands across his forehead.

He looked up, saw me, and his mood darkened.

"Close the door," he ordered.

I shut it with a trembling hand.

He stood up and walked over to me.

His massive chest rippled, and his abs cast shadows from the bright light of the windows.

He had all sorts of tattoos: black swirling patterns, guns, skulls, phrases in Italian like 'Family Above All.'

They seemed dangerous... mysterious... and I stared at them in wonder.

Well... actually, I was staring at his gorgeous body, and the tattoos just happened to be there.

He stopped right in front of me and looked down. Even in his bare feet, he towered above me.

"You came into my room earlier," he said.

It wasn't a question.

"...yes," I admitted.

"What did Niccolo tell you about the eastern wing of the second floor?"

"But Caterina was going to deliver your breakfast, and she was busy," I lied, "and she wanted me to help her – "

Dario put up a hand. I stopped talking immediately.

"What did Niccolo tell you about the eastern wing of the second floor?"

I cast my eyes down at the floor. "...not to come here."

"And yet you did."

"...yes."

"And then you looked in at me while I was in the shower."

My eyes flew up to his face in a panic.

He was staring at me angrily.

"...yes," I whispered and looked back down at the floor.

"Do you do that a lot? Spy on people?"

"No," I protested, even as I guiltily thought of Caterina and Valentino the other day.

Dario grabbed my chin roughly and lifted my face. "Look at me."

I stared into his dark eyes. I could barely breathe.

"You watched me while I was naked," he said.

I bit my lower lip and nodded mutely.

"Then I think it's only fair I see *you* naked," he said.

My eyes grew wide. "Dario – "

"DON Rosolini to you."

"...Don... Rosolini..."

"Yes?"

"Please... I don't..."

"It wasn't a question," he said, his voice deep and smoky.

My heart was thudding in my chest...

My face felt scorching hot...

And between my legs, I felt the same throbbing desire as last night.

But I just stood there staring into his eyes.

He kept his right hand on my chin, forcing me to look up at him...

And with his left hand, he started to undo the buttons that went down the front of my dress.

"No," I whispered.

"You said that last night," he growled. "Did it change anything?"

I didn't answer.

I just kept staring into his eyes like I was hypnotized.

One button was already undone, down to my collarbone.

I felt him do the next...

Then the next...

Until his knuckles grazed my breast.

I drew in a sharp breath.

He continued to undo the buttons one by one until the front of my dress was slightly open all the way to my stomach.

Then he gently slid my dress off my left shoulder.

"Please, don't," I whispered, my voice trembling.

He ignored me and slipped the cloth off my right shoulder.

My dress dropped into a pile at my feet.

I didn't have a bra on, only my panties...

So I was standing there almost completely naked before him.

I closed my eyes.

My entire body was on fire... and yet I wanted to be consumed by it.

His hand left my face, and suddenly I felt his rough fingers on my back...

Tracing my spine...

Down to my ass.

His fingers grasped my panties and slid them down my thighs.

As he did it, his body touched me –

His hot, damp skin brushing against mine –

His hard muscles pressing against my breasts.

I moaned as I felt him...

And wanted to feel *so much more.*

Seconds later, his lips were on mine.

Soft...

Sensual...

And as he kissed me, his hands touched me everywhere.

*All* over my body.

Gliding down my arms...

Caressing my back...

Cupping my ass...

One hand gently stroking my right breast...

Making my firm nipple even harder...

And then gliding down to the thatch of hair between my legs.

I felt drunk...

Swooning...

And I lifted my hands for the first time to touch *him.*

I could only touch him because my eyes were closed. That way I didn't have to watch myself sin.

My fingers glided over his massive shoulders...

The rippling muscles of his back...

I even traced my fingers across his rock-hard abs.

Then he pressed himself against me, and I felt something hard.

I broke off from the kiss so I could look down.

Inside his pants, his...

His *cock*...

Was huge and stiff as it jutted at an angle to the side.

My jaw dropped open as I stared at it.

No matter how big his cock had looked when it was dangling in the shower, it was *so* much bigger now, even though it was still hidden beneath his slacks.

*So THAT was what Cat meant about it getting hard...*

I reached out a trembling hand and touched it...

Cupped it with my palm...

Ran my fingers down the length of it...

Held it tight in my grasp.

I could feel the heat of it radiating through the cloth.

Dario groaned –

And then suddenly he picked me up and swept me off my feet.

One arm supported my back, while the other was under the bend of my knees.

I cried out in surprise.

Before I knew it, he had walked over to the bed and thrown me down on the silken sheets.

Their touch on my naked skin felt delicious.

I also couldn't believe how good it felt to be picked up by a strong man and tossed like it was nothing.

But when I looked at Dario's face, I was frightened –

Because he seemed absolutely insane with desire.

He loomed over me –

And then suddenly he lowered his head between my legs.

I gasped as I felt his beard along the inside of my legs –

And then he kissed the lips of my pussy.

I groaned and closed my eyes.

It felt *so good* –

And then it got ten times better.

He began to lick me... my legs at first, and then my lips...

And finally the hot little button of pleasure he had touched last night.

My clit...

His tongue circled it gently.

"OH MY GOD," I cried out as I grabbed his head and gripped his wet hair with my fingers.

He licked me so softly, so sweetly –

His hot tongue wet against my clit –

And then the pressure built like it had last night.

Faster, firmer, hotter, wetter –

And I began to come.

My back arched as the first waves of pleasure rolled through me from head to toe.

I screamed out loud as he continued to lick.

The pleasure just built, and built, and built –

And I screamed some more as I thrashed my body on his silk sheets.

It went on for several minutes: me thinking I had hit a new peak of pleasure, only to be taken higher.

But gradually the waves began to subside.

I stopped moaning and wriggling...

And his tongue withdrew from my clit.

I felt a little disappointed –

Until I felt something new.

Something *amazing.*

His tongue was parting my lips...

And moving inside me.

I gasped.

It was wet and hot and incredible...

And it sparked a hunger to take *more* inside me, to feel completely filled up.

His tongue was just teasing me...

I wanted more. *So* much more.

"Dario," I gasped.

He stopped what he was doing and said, "What?"

I swallowed hard... then said in a tremulous voice, "Can I see it?"

I had a throbbing need – a desperate desire that wouldn't go away until satisfied.

"I just... want to see it," I whispered.

He backed away from the bed and stood. "Come and do it your-self, then."

I felt a mixture of shame and overwhelming desire.

Desire won out.

I scooted to the edge of the bed and put my palms flat against his magnificent abs.

Then I looked up at him.

He smiled down at me. "...well?"

I bit my lower lip... then fumbled with his pants.

I undid the button in the waistband... then I pulled down the zipper.

He wasn't wearing any underwear.

As soon I saw the thatch of curly dark hair at the bottom of his abs, my mouth began to water.

I slowly tugged his pants down. It was difficult because his cock was at an angle, and I had to get the pants down over it –

But what little I saw made me even hungrier.

The base of his cock was *very* thick...

And *very* hard...

And with veins that stood up underneath his skin.

I slowly slid the pants down, watching as more of his shaft was exposed...

Until finally the material slid over the end and his entire cock was freed.

I gasped as it sprang up in the air.

The head was bulbous and huge...

And there was a beautiful upward curve to it.

The size of him...

The masculinity of his body... of his cock...

I had never felt more feminine in my entire life.

I wanted to touch it *so bad.*

I put out a tentative hand, then drew back.

I looked up at him as though asking permission...

And he nodded.

I reached out again...

And this time took his cock in my hand.

I moaned involuntarily.

The skin was so soft...

But just underneath, it was hard as stone.

And *so* hot to the touch.

I slowly traced my hand up and down its length...

And he grunted.

I felt his cock spasm once in my hand. It grew the tiniest bit in size, just for an instant.

The swollen head expanded just a bit –

And a tiny bead of clear liquid seeped out from the slit in the swollen head.

I stared at it in wonder...

And without thinking, I leaned forward and put my lips around the tip to taste it.

It was salty... but I loved the taste.

And I loved how slippery it was on my lips.

I kissed his cock softly...

And he groaned.

I looked up to see him with his head flung back, the cords in his neck tight.

He *liked* it.

I grinned and began to kiss him some more... slowly... delicately...

While I slowly caressed him with my fingers, gently running my hand up and down the length of his shaft.

Suddenly he stepped back, which pulled his cock out of my grasp.

I felt indignant, like he had taken away the thing I wanted most –

And then his strong hands lifted me up in the air and threw me effortlessly back on the bed.

I shrieked in surprise and delight as I landed on my back –

Then watched lustfully as he crawled up on the bed, his cock jutting up in the air towards me.

I realized what he intended, and suddenly I was filled with fear.

"Dario... no..." I whispered.

He ignored me and pried my legs apart – and then positioned himself between them.

"Dario, no!" I whimpered.

"Quiet," he growled.

He took his cock in his hand and guided it towards my pussy.

My entire body tensed as I waited for him to enter me –

But he didn't.

Instead, he put the underside of his cock between the lips of my pussy, parting them, and began to slide up and down the full length of his shaft.

The underside of his cock grew slick from my wetness –

And suddenly his bare skin was gliding over my clit.

It felt *amazing*.

I cried out as he moved back and forth – his hard cock sliding wetly across my clit – up, up, up, then down, down, down.

"I told you I wouldn't take you until you begged me," he murmured in my ear. "But I also said I was going to do everything *else* to you that I wanted."

The pressure of his wet cock across my clit intensified.

I gasped in pleasure and raked my fingers across his shoulders.

Then he began to kiss me – and I passionately kissed him back –

All while he was thrusting between my legs and rubbing his cock across my clit.

I began to come less than 30 seconds later...

But this time, every slippery stroke across my clit lasted a couple of seconds and made me go higher and higher with pleasure.

His cock pressed even *more* firmly into me –

And I came even harder.

I didn't know where one orgasm ended and another began as they all overlapped.

I couldn't contain myself. I screamed at the top of my lungs.

Suddenly *he* was bellowing like a bull –

And I felt something hot and wet squirt across my belly and breasts.

I looked down in time to see white liquid spurt from the end of his cock.

It made me even *more* lustful – and the sight of his orgasm and the sounds of his pleasure made me come even harder.

Gradually his thrusts slowed and stopped... but my own waves of ecstasy had subsided by then.

Dario grunted and rolled off me to the side...

But one of his hands still caressed my body.

"Did that feel... good for you?" I asked timidly.

He grinned. "Amazing."

He looked at the white liquid on my belly and breasts and said, "Looks like you need a shower. Come on."

And then he pulled me up by the hand and led me to the bathroom.

# 24

Dario

That morning with Alessandra was perhaps the greatest two hours of my life.

The way she made me feel...

Her beautiful body...

The overwhelming release when I came...

The way her innocent face looked when *she* came...

Everything about my time with her had been astounding.

The shower afterwards had been long and luxurious, with plenty of kissing and fondling her breasts as water cascaded over her body.

Once we got out, I dried her off... had her put on her dress...

And sent her on her way with a slap on her ass.

Her innocent brown eyes had been filled with surprise –

But she'd liked it.

And I knew immediately what I would do to her the next time I took her to bed.

I still hadn't fucked her – not properly – but that would come soon.

I was going to have to break her in first. There was no way she would be able to handle me without pain unless I did.

But there was time... and I was looking forward to it.

In fact, I was happier than I could ever remember being.

But not everyone else was.

"Have you lost your fucking mind?" Niccolo shouted in my study. "The rest of the house could hear her screaming! The entire staff is talking!"

"Let them talk," I said coldly. "I pay their wages, not the other way around."

"It's not just that. We have a *visitor* this afternoon. Or did you forget?"

"No," I snapped.

Although, to be truthful, I *had* forgotten.

Being with a beautiful naked woman for hours will do that do you.

"I need you to be in top form for this," Niccolo said. "Not distracted."

*"Consigliere,"* I snapped.

Niccolo gritted his teeth. "...what."

"I am your *don*. I suggest you remember that."

Niccolo looked resentful for a second, then got ahold of himself. "At least let me get her out of the house while our guest is here."

"Why?"

Niccolo knew better than to voice the real reason, which I already knew:

I wanted to fuck her – and I might just rush through the meeting so I could get her back into bed.

"We don't need her causing any commotion during the talks," Niccolo said. "Sneaking out again like she did yesterday."

"She won't."

"Nonetheless, I want her out of the house."

I scowled at him... but he was probably right. If Alessandra wasn't here, it *would* make it easier to focus.

"What did you have in mind?" I asked.

"Have Massimo and Valentino take her to Florence for the rest of the day. She can do some shopping, and they can all have dinner."

I narrowed my eyes. "You're not worried about our enemies?"

"Florence is a big city. I doubt it will be a problem."

"You '*doubt*' it will be a problem?"

Niccolo sighed. "Aren't you the least bit worried about the Turk?"

'The Turk' was Mehmet Erdogan, a member of an organized crime cartel from Turkey who wanted to discuss business. Our uncle had put him in contact with us.

"Fausto vouched for him," I pointed out.

"Yes, well, until we find out why the Genoans are trying to horn in on our territory – and why they sent the spy that Lars killed – and why the hell we have a dead priest and a thug buried in the orchards out back – I'm not trusting *anyone,* not even if Saint Peter himself says they're alright."

"Where are we on finding out who the priest and the other one are?"

"Our friends at the *Questura* are running their fingerprints for us."

"Let me know when you find something out."

"Of course."

I sighed. "Alright... send in Alessandra so I can tell her about Florence."

"OHHHH no – *I'll* tell her," Niccolo said as he walked to the door. "I don't need you getting distracted and banging her for the next two hours. I *certainly* don't need her screaming when the Turk arrives."

I just smirked as he left the room.

The meeting with the Turk was a courtesy to our uncle, nothing more... and I might have been tempted to blow it off in order to spend a little more time with Alessandra.

Probably best to listen to my *consigliere* for once.

## 25

Alessandra

Niccolo came up to my room an hour after I left Dario.

I was still walking around with a huge smile on my face when the *consigliere* knocked on the door.

"We have an important meeting this afternoon," Niccolo said, "and I need you out of the house. Massimo and Valentino will take you to Florence where you can do some shopping and get some new clothes. Buy whatever you want – Massimo will pay for it. You'll have dinner in Florence and come back later this evening."

Yesterday morning, Niccolo's news would have been incredibly welcome.

A chance to leave the house and perhaps sneak away?

Yes, please!

But now I was just overwhelmed with anxiety.

"Is Dario... displeased with me?" I asked nervously.

"No, although *I* am," Niccolo said. "I'd prefer it if you could be a bit quieter when you have an orgasm. We can hear you on the other side of the house."

My face immediately turned scarlet, and I felt like I might die right there on the spot.

I'd been so overcome with passion when I was with Dario that I hadn't even considered that anyone else could hear me.

Niccolo laughed at my reaction. "Don't worry, nobody's judging you. Well, not me, anyway – or any of my brothers or Lars. Valentino's probably happy because you're making Caterina even hornier."

I stared at him in horror. "You know about that?!"

"I know about *everything* that goes on this house," he said ominously. "Now go get ready. You'll be leaving right away."

I left with Massimo and Valentino exactly 15 minutes later.

And as I passed by Filomena in the foyer, I stared at the ground in shame...

Because I could not meet her disapproving gaze.

## 26

The trip to Florence took an hour. Valentino drove the Mercedes, and Massimo sat in the passenger seat up front. He was so tall that he had to move the seat all the way back – and yet he *still* looked cramped.

I sat in the backseat and watched the scenery go by.

The landscape of Tuscany was truly beautiful. Wheat fields that rippled in the wind... silver-green olive groves... the occasional patch of red poppies or yellow sunflowers.

There were sprawling vineyards with their orderly rows of grape vines...

Cypress trees, tall and slender...

Ancient farmhouses of terracotta and stone...

And every so often there was a castle on a hilltop, straight out of a fairy tale.

But eventually I got bored. After all, I had grown up among all of this... even if I had never seen it while riding in a car.

So instead, I started up a conversation with Massimo and Valentino.

"Tell me," I said, "whose idea was this little trip?"

Massimo shrugged. "Does it matter?"

"I'd like to know who wanted me out of the house."

I could see Valentino's smirk in the rearview mirror. "Well, it definitely wasn't *Dario* who wanted you gone."

My face flushed bright red as I remembered Niccolo's comments about my screaming being audible throughout the house.

"You're awful!" I said with embarrassment, indignation, and a little bit of humor.

He just laughed.

"Besides, *you're* one to talk," I shot back.

"How's that?"

"I know what you do with Caterina."

Massimo snorted. *"Everyone* knows what he does with Caterina."

"At least you can't hear her through the entire house," Valentino said with a pointed look at me in the mirror.

I burned bright red –

Until Massimo came to my rescue.

"Maybe you're not *good enough* to make her scream that loud," he said to Valentino.

I stifled a giggle.

I knew it wasn't true – I'd seen Caterina biting Valentino's shoulder to stifle her cries of passion – but it was funny to hear.

Plus, I wasn't about to admit I'd seen Caterina and Valentino having sex.

"Fuck you!" Valentino said playfully as he smacked his brother in the arm.

"The only reason I'm not hitting you back is because you're driving," Massimo said.

"So?"

"So you're a bad enough driver as it is. I don't want to die because you're worse at driving than you are in bed."

"You fucking asshole!" Valentino said, laughing out loud. "Who are *you* to talk to me about pleasing my woman? The monk who hasn't gotten laid in over a year – "

"I could take over for you if you like," Massimo suggested. "Then we'd see how loud your woman can scream."

"Don't even *think* about it, or I'll kill you," Valentino said, somewhere between joking and serious.

"If you don't kill me with your driving first – stay in the right lane, *rimbambito!*" Massimo snapped, using a slang term for *numbnuts.*

By the time we got to Florence, I was talking and joking with the two brothers like old friends.

We drove through the newer parts of the city, past dingy buildings from the last 70 years. Then we got to old Florence – the section that had stood for over six centuries.

Massimo guided the Mercedes through the maze of streets until we reached the *Via dè Tornabuoni,* the most famous street for shopping in all of Tuscany. It was the Florentine equivalent of Rodeo Drive in Los Angeles. Boutiques for Gucci, Balenciaga, Hermes, Prada, and Tiffany lined the streets.

"Oh my goodness," I whispered as Massimo parked the car in front of the Versace store. "Isn't there somewhere else you can take me – like H&M?"

Massimo snorted. "If I bring you back to Dario wearing H&M, he'll castrate me."

"Your balls are so small already, it's no great loss," Valentino joked.

"I'll make sure he takes yours, too."

"Hey – I actually *use* mine!"

I looked down at my dowdy dress. "But... I'm not dressed to go in there!"

"Yeah, but *we* are," Massimo said, straightening the lapels of his expensive suit.

"Stick with us, Alessandra," Valentino said with a wink and a smile. "We'll *take* you places."

The three of us walked into the store. Massimo and Valentino acted like they owned the place, while *I* felt like a peasant walking into a palace.

A very stylish woman about 10 years older than me walked over. "Good afternoon, gentlemen – how can I help you today?"

"Dress this woman beautifully and spare no expense," Massimo said.

"Done," the woman said with a smile. "And for you?"

"We're fine."

"You're not wearing Versace, though," she pointed out.

"No – Armani."

"Well, I won't hold it against you," she said in an amused voice.

I was about to follow her when I made the mistake of looking at a price tag on a blouse.

It was 700 euros – about $750 US.

"We can't buy anything from here!" I whispered in a panic to Massimo.

"Why not?" he asked, and looked around in surprise. "Too ugly?"

"No, it's all beautiful – it's just too expensive!"

"*What's* too expensive?"

I showed him the price tag of 700 euros.

"Wait – hold on for a moment," Massimo said.

Then he proceeded to stare at me with a bored face.

I waited for about 20 seconds before I asked, "What am I waiting for, exactly?"

"THAT," he said as he punctuated the air with a stab of his finger.

"...what?" I asked, mystified.

"That's how long it takes for our family to make 700 euros."

My eyes went wide. "It *is?*"

"That's not true," Valentino said to Massimo. "That'd be over a thousand euros a minute – 60,000 euros an hour! That's a million dollars a day – 356 million a year – "

"Shut up," Massimo told Valentino, then turned back to me. "I'm hungry. Go buy some clothes so we can get out of here and eat."

The saleswoman had me try on dress after gorgeous dress. Massimo watched me every time I came out, though whenever I asked his opinion, he would only say, "It's nice." Occasionally he would throw in a "Get whatever you want."

Valentino got bored after the first dress and proceeded to flirt with every pretty woman in the store.

I got irritated with him on Caterina's behalf but held my tongue.

I finally settled on a couple of subdued dresses that were still absolutely beautiful – one in emerald green and another in rose. I also got two blouses and two patterned skirts.

"That's it?" Massimo asked when I brought him the clothes.

"'That's *it*'?!" I exclaimed in a whisper. "All of these together are over 6000 euros!"

He picked up a couple of items I'd had trouble deciding on. I'd eventually discarded them because of the price.

"Do you like these?" he asked.

"Yes, but – "

Massimo handed them to the saleslady along with a black credit card. "Ring these up, too."

"Gladly," she said as she took everything to the register.

"Massimo!" I exclaimed.

"What?"

"I can't accept these things!"

"Yes, you can."

"No, I can't!"

"Yes you *can*, because I like my balls where they are."

"I thought he'd only castrate you if I came back wearing H&M."

"If he finds out I didn't let you buy as much as you wanted because of the price, he'll probably take my pecker, too."

Once the items were paid for and packed up, Massimo carried a bag in each hand. He made Valentino take the rest as we exited onto the street.

"I can carry them," I protested.

He refused. "You're a lady. Ladies don't carry packages when there are gentlemen present."

"I'm not a gentleman," Valentino said with a smile, "so I shouldn't have to carry them."

"Shut up, pack mule," Massimo replied affably, then licked his chops. "Now... where to eat?"

## 27

Dario

The Turk arrived three hours after Alessandra and my brothers left.

I watched from a window as he drove up in a small convoy of BMWs. When he got out of his car, two bodyguards flanked him on either side. Everyone else stayed in their vehicles.

I had instructed my men – the low-level foot soldiers who guarded the estate – to search them for weapons. Only once they were determined to be clean were they allowed inside.

Niccolo met them at the front door. Then he brought the Turk alone into the study where Roberto, Adriano, and I were waiting.

Lars wasn't with us. He was stationed on the roof, waiting with his sniper rifle...

Just in case the Turk's men got a bit unruly.

"Mr. Erdogan," I said as I shook his hand.

"Don Rosolini," the Turk said. He was an older man, probably 45, tall and impeccably dressed in a suit. He would have been handsome if not for the jagged scar that ran from his left ear to the corner of his mouth. "I have to say, I'm not used to being frisked like some common thug at a nightclub."

His comment irked me. I wondered if that was the intended effect.

"Security is our highest priority," I said coolly as we all sat down. "I'm sure you understand."

"I know your uncle trusts me," the Turk replied in his heavily accented Italian.

"In *this* house, trust is earned. What can I do for you today."

"Straight to business, eh?" he said with a grin that was made sinister by his scar. "Fausto said you would get right down to brass tacks."

"I don't want to waste my time *or* yours."

Niccolo gave me a disapproving look, but I disliked the man's demeanor. There was a lack of respect in his tone that I found irritating.

My father wouldn't have stood for it... and if Fausto did, then he was a fool – even if he *was* my uncle.

The Turk nodded. "Alright, here it is: we're doing business with the Agrella family in Florence."

The Agrellas were a rival family that ruled over most of Florence.

However, *we* were the ones with the politicians and judges in our pocket.

The Agrellas ran the streets; the Rosolinis controlled the halls of government.

Our families had observed an uneasy alliance for over 20 years. It had never once been violated in all that time.

The Turk continued. "But, as we both know, I must go through *your* territory in Tuscany to deliver my goods to the Agrellas. I'd like to leverage your connections to move my wares into Florence, for which you would receive a 10% cut of revenue. If there were additional issues I needed handling – say, bribing a judge or the police – I would be willing to negotiate those on a case-by-case basis."

"10% is a bit low," Roberto said. "We'd normally charge 20%."

"That was understandable when your father was alive," the Turk replied. "But since his death, I have to wonder if 20% is really worth it."

His words were beyond rude.

Adriano, hothead that he was, leapt to his feet. *"Vaffanculo, pezzo di merda!"*

*Fuck you, piece of shit!*

The Turk raised his hands. "I did not mean to give offense. My Italian is not the best. I was simply stating what I see as the reality of the situation."

"The reality of the situation," Niccolo said coldly, "doesn't include insulting our family."

"Am I, though? After your father's death, the family's territory was split between you and your uncle, no? So the once-formidable Rosolini empire is now broken in two. Am I incorrect in stating it thus?" the Turk said, his choice of words a bit stiff and formal.

Adriano, Niccolo, and Roberto looked at me to see my reaction.

I kept my temper. I already disliked the Turk, but I wasn't going to quibble over percentages. Not when there were far more pressing questions.

"I'm more interested in exactly what kind of 'wares' you'll be providing to the Agrellas," I said.

"Drugs, for one," the Turk said. "We have opium and heroin from Turkey, plus I have a connection from South America for cocaine. And we have methamphetamine labs throughout Serbia and Croatia. Then there are the girls we bring in from Eastern Europe – "

"I can stop you right there," I said coldly. "We don't deal with sex trafficking anymore, and we're out of the drug trade as well."

The Turk looked at me as though I'd gone insane. "Since when?"

"Since the death of my father and the empire was broken in two," I said sardonically.

"But... your father dealt in all those things – I *know* he did – "

"Yes, well, today is a new day, I am the new don of the family, and we choose not to sully our hands."

The Turk's cheeks flushed with anger. "Are you saying *my* hands are sullied, then?"

"What – am I incorrect in stating it thus?" I asked sarcastically as I threw his own words back in his face.

The Turk's voice grew colder. "If I may be so bold – if you are completely out of the sex and drug trade, then what *do* you deal in?"

I gestured at Roberto to take over.

He nodded and turned to the Turk. "As you stated earlier, our primary strengths are political influence and our connections in the police and court system. We also control ports along the western coast, including the smuggling of stolen goods. Then there's gambling, which we intend to make our main source of revenue over the next two years."

"Gambling," the Turk scoffed. "That's nowhere near as big as what *I* can offer you."

"*We'll* worry about that," I said. "As you can see, your aims are incompatible with ours... which means we won't be doing business."

"How am I supposed to get my goods into Florence?" the Turk snarled.

"Fly them in. I don't control the airways."

"Look, all I need is land transportation – "

"If the Agrellas want to hire local girls to be sex workers, I can't control that," I snapped. "But you *won't* be trafficking women across *my* territory. The same goes for drugs."

The Turk shook his head and scoffed. "Your uncle *said* you'd gone soft."

My anger grew even hotter when I heard his words.

Whatever disagreements Fausto and I had had in the past, my uncle should have *never* spoken against family like that.

"Yes, well, perhaps you should do business with *him*," I said coldly. "I think that concludes our business for today."

The Turk scowled. "No, it *doesn't* – "

I stared him down. "*Yes,* it DOES. My brother will show you out. Adriano?"

"With pleasure," Adriano said as he walked over to the Turk's chair.

"You're passing up a major opportunity there," the Turk snarled.

"Oh well."

The Turk shook his head. "Unbelievable."

"Believe it."

Adriano started to take the man's arm, but the Turk jerked it away and rose on his own. Then he walked out of the room with Adriano following close behind.

"Well, *that* was interesting," Niccolo said after they'd left.

"Are you getting the same feeling that I am?" I asked.

"That this wasn't about doing business with us, but sizing us up to see if he wants to make a move?" Niccolo said. "Absolutely."

"If Fausto actually said that about us going soft, we need to have a talk with him," Roberto said.

"I was thinking the exact same thing," I muttered. "Niccolo, call our 'dear uncle' and arrange something for tomorrow."

# 28

Alessandra

W e ate lunch at a beautiful restaurant in old Florence. The tables were set with white linen and crystal glasses, and the food was amazing.

"The only time I've eaten a better meal was at your house," I told Massimo.

He patted his full belly. "Two out of two experts agree."

"You gotta admit, though," Valentino said, "that place in Rome we go to is better."

"Hey – the lady just applauded our cooks at home," Massimo said good-naturedly. "Take the compliment, huh?"

"I would *hope* you think certain things are better at home," I told Valentino with a trace of irritation in my voice.

"Uh-oh, sounds like I'm in trouble," Valentino said.

"Sounds like it," Massimo agreed.

"What'd I do, exactly?" Valentino asked me.

"You were flirting with every woman in the store when you've got a wonderful woman at home."

"Ah," Valentino said as though he finally understood. "Look, Caterina went into this with eyes wide open. I never lied to her. She knows what I am."

"And what's that?" I asked in a deadpan voice.

"A man-whore," Massimo answered.

I laughed.

Valentino held out his arms like, *What can I do?* "I am what I am and I want what I want."

"And what do you want?"

*"Everything,"* he said with a grin.

"I hope you're not including me in 'everything,'" I said coolly.

Valentino raised a finger like he had forgotten something. "I meant to say, 'Everything that wouldn't kill me if I got it.'"

"What, you're saying *I'd* kill you?"

"No – Dario would," Valentino said. "And that's the truth."

I made a face like I didn't believe him.

"Dario's very protective of you," Massimo agreed.

"I thought he was just very... possessive," I said darkly.

"Dario doesn't care about much. But what he *does* care about, he guards with his life."

"Why did he kick me out of the house, then?"

"'Why did he kick me out,'" Valentino said, gently mocking me. "A couple of days ago, you risked everything to *leave.*"

"Well..." I said, not wanting to admit he had a point.

"Ha – you *know* I'm right."

"That doesn't explain why he sent me away."

"There was a meeting with a potential business partner," Massimo explained. "I suppose he wanted..."

Then he trailed off.

"What did he want?" I asked.

Massimo and Valentino looked at each other, then laughed.

"What's so funny?" I demanded.

"I can't even lie," Valentino said with a grin. *"Dario* didn't want you gone – "

"Niccolo did," I finished.

"Yup."

"But why?"

"Probably for the same reason he only lets Caterina work half a day," Massimo said.

"And why's that?"

"So Valentino isn't slipping off to fuck her every chance he gets. He only gets to do it in the mornings."

"Oh my god!" I cried.

"What, your virgin ears can't take the truth?" Valentino said with a laugh. Then he suddenly acted serious and put his hands over the sides of his head. "*My* virgin ears can't take your screaming when you and Dario get together."

I turned bright red and hid my eyes with my hand.

Massimo laughed but scolded Valentino at the same time. "Stop teasing her."

"Oh my god, oh my god, oh my god..." I murmured, mortified.

Valentino howled with laughter. "Funny, that's what you say with Dario – just louder and higher-pitched. 'Oh my god, oh my GOD – '"

"STOP IT!" I cried out as I threw a dinner roll at him.

"No food fights, children," Massimo chided us playfully.

"Yes, Dad," I said, half-joking and half-annoyed.

"The truth is, we're glad you're with him," Massimo said.

"Can we *please* stop talking about this?" I begged.

"I'm talking about in a *general* sense. Not in a Valentino kind of way."

"What, sex in the kitchen pantry?" Valentino asked.

Massimo made a face. "You do it near the food? Come ON, man..."

"PLEASE can we stop talking about this!" I whispered.

"Alright, alright. But I *am* glad you're here," Massimo said. "At the house, I mean."

"Why?"

Massimo smiled. "Because I've never seen my brother happier."

## 29

*'ve never seen my brother happier.*

I thought about Massimo's words as we made our way back to the car.

Part of me was elated...

...but part of me was confused.

Dario was still frightening to me in many ways.

He was also a complete enigma.

He seemed like he was angry with me half the time...

...and the other half, he seemed like he was obsessed.

I started thinking about the second half...

And what he had done to me that morning...

When Massimo put a hand on my back and pushed me gently through the street.

"Go faster," he whispered.

"What?" I asked as I came out of my daydream.

I was about to ask him why when I noticed that he and Valentino were looking around furtively.

"What's going on?" I whispered.

"Something's not right," Massimo muttered as he looked around.

The street was busy with pedestrians on the sidewalks – but something seemed wrong.

It was like a picture where one thing was out of place. You could sense something was off, but you couldn't quite put your finger on it.

"Get to the car and open the back door," Massimo ordered Valentino.

Valentino took off at a sprint –

Which may have been what triggered our enemies to finally reveal themselves –

Like they were afraid they'd been found out.

Two men across the street darted out into traffic, weapons drawn.

"DOWN!" Massimo shouted as he pushed me behind a parked car and drew his own gun from the back of his pants.

The two men shot at us from the street.

*BANG BANG BANG BANG BANG!*

Glass shattered –

Cars screeched to a halt –

People screamed and scattered all around us –

And Massimo returned fire.

*BANG BANG BANG!*

"STAY DOWN!" Valentino shouted as he fired his own gun over our heads.

I looked to my right and saw a third man collapse. A pistol fell from his hand to the sidewalk.

Massimo fired another shot to make sure the stranger was dead, then turned back to the two gunmen in the street.

He shot one man –

And the other ducked down behind a car.

Massimo pulled me to my feet and shouted, "RUN!"

He stayed between me and the gunman the entire way, acting as a shield to keep me safe.

Fifty feet up ahead, Valentino was shooting at someone else I couldn't see. He continued to fire as he flung open the back door of the Mercedes and circled around to the driver's side.

There were gunshots everywhere –

Glass storefronts shattered –

And suddenly we were at the car.

"GET IN, GET IN!" Massimo bellowed.

I scrambled into the back seat.

Massimo shot a final round before diving in behind me and slamming the door shut.

Valentino was already in the driver's seat and starting the engine.

The window next to me exploded with a spider-web of cracks, and there was a metallic *ping ping ping!* as bullets hit the car door.

I screamed – then realized that nothing was getting through.

The car was bulletproof.

"GET US OUT OF HERE!" Massimo yelled.

Valentino swerved around stopped cars and took a hard left at top speed.

"Are you alright?!" Massimo asked me frantically.

"Yes!" I said. I was terrified, but I didn't feel pain anywhere.

"Val?" Massimo asked.

"I'm good – you alright?"

"I got nicked," Massimo said with a grimace.

Only then did I see the blood on his shirt beneath his jacket.

"Oh my god!" I cried out.

"It's fine, it's not bad," he told me.

"How do you know?!"

He gave a wry smile. "I've been shot before. This is nothing."

"Should I go to the hospital?" Valentino asked.

"Fuck no – just get us out of the city," Massimo said as he pulled out a phone. "I'll let Niccolo know what's going on. He'll tell us what to do."

# 30

Dario

I was still brooding over the Turk's visit an hour after the Turk left.

I was sitting in my study when Niccolo walked in, his face pale.

"What's wrong?" I asked.

"There was a shooting in Florence," he replied.

For the first time in a long while, I felt fear –

Panic.

"Alessandra?!" I asked as I bolted up from my chair.

"She's fine," Niccolo said, then added drily, "although your concern for your brothers is touching."

I gave him a look like *Don't fuck with me right now.* "Are they alright?"

"Valentino is. Massimo was shot."

I stared at him. "How bad is it?"

"He says it's through-and-through, no severe damage – but I'm having them meet a gunshot doctor at a safe house run by the Agrellas."

"NO. Tell him to get back here *now*."

Niccolo looked angry. "If this is about protecting Alessandra – "

"How do we know the Agrellas weren't behind the hit?"

"We don't, but they – "

"Haven't violated our arrangement in over 20 years – is that what you were going to say?"

"Let me guess what *you're* going to say," Niccolo snapped. "That it's incredibly suspicious the Agrellas are doing business with the man you just turned down an hour ago."

"If it's a coincidence, it's the worst one I've ever seen. Do we know where the Turk's base of operations is?"

Niccolo shook his head. "No – and his car is probably out of reach by now."

"The Agrellas aren't," I snarled. "We know *exactly* where they are."

"The Agrellas *could* have hired some out-of-town hitters to take out Valentino and Massimo, it's true," Niccolo admitted. "Or they might have agreed to let the Turk's men take a shot. Either is possible – but I just spoke to the Agrellas' *consigliere,* and he offered us one of their safe houses. If their family does something out in the open that hurts Massimo or Valentino, it's full-out war. The Agrellas aren't stupid enough to risk that."

"Unless they're like the Turk and think Papa's death made us weak," I said. "Are you really going to bet Massimo and Valentino's lives on that?"

Niccolo narrowed his eyes. "And Alessandra's life, too? Or did you just conveniently leave her name out?"

"Get them back here *immediately*. Call the cops to make sure they're not stopped. Get them a new car if theirs is shot up. Do whatever it takes – but we're *not* trusting the Agrellas on this."

Niccolo shook his head as he pulled out his phone and dialed. "Prison made you paranoid – you know that?"

"If you're going to be a wartime *consigliere,* brother, you had better get a lot *more* paranoid," I snapped.

Niccolo glared at me, then turned away. "Massimo? New plan..."

# 31

Alessandra

Lars and ten of the family's foot soldiers met us halfway back to the house. They were waiting in three new cars by the side of the road, and most of the men were heavily armed.

There was a man with them who was apparently a doctor. While Lars kept guard, the doctor checked out Massimo and hooked up an IV and bag of saline to his arm. Then he cut open Massimo's shirt with a razor so he could inspect the wound.

"Is he going to be alright?" I asked anxiously.

"No more shootouts for a while, but he'll be fine," the doctor assured me. "The bullet didn't even go through a muscle – basically just through skin and fat."

"Hey – are you calling me fat?" Massimo said with fake umbrage.

Lars grinned. "Don't worry. We know you're just big-boned."

While the doctor bandaged up Massimo, everyone talked by the roadside.

"Thank you," I told Massimo for the dozenth time.

He gave me a lopsided smile. "Eh, it was nothing."

"You saved my life. That's not 'nothing.'"

"Hey, *I* got the car," Valentino said humorously. "I'd just like to point out we'd *all* be dead if it wasn't for that."

"Thank you, too," I said, playing along.

"It's nothing," he said with jokey fake modesty. "Just as long as everybody realizes who the *real* hero is."

"Fuck you," Massimo said with a laugh. "You didn't get shot."

"Yeah, because I was smart enough *not* to."

"If intelligence kept a man from getting shot, you would have gotten your brains blown out."

Valentino grinned. "Probably."

"And there wouldn't have been a noticeable difference in your IQ, either," Massimo joked.

"Hey – as long as they didn't shoot off my dick."

"Gotta have your priorities straight," Lars said with a grin.

"Actually," Valentino said, "my theory is I didn't get shot because I'm not as big of a target as Massimo."

"Is that so," Massimo said sarcastically.

Valentino pointed at me. "Tiny target – didn't get shot."

Then he pointed at himself. "Bigger target – didn't get shot."

Then he pointed at Massimo. "Gigantic fucking target – got shot. I'd say the conclusion is obvious."

"I think it's because you run as fast as a frightened little squirrel," Massimo said.

"That could be part of it," Valentino agreed. Then he grinned and pointed at his face. "But I *had* to run fast – gotta keep this pretty for the ladies."

"You're saying I'm not pretty?" Massimo asked.

"Let's just say that a couple of bullets to the face might improve your appearance."

Once the doctor said Massimo was okay, Valentino, Lars, Massimo, and I got into a limousine. One of the foot soldiers drove the bullet-riddled Mercedes back to the mansion.

"This is serious, you know," Lars said to Massimo as we all rode in the back of the limo.

"I know," Massimo replied.

"What, you getting shot up?" I said facetiously. I was amazed they were so blasé about it. "I'd say it's just a *little* bit serious."

"No, not that," Massimo said. "Niccolo arranged for us to go to a safe house run by another family – but then he called back and said no, come back to the mansion instead."

"Which means...?"

"Which means he doesn't trust our allies in Florence," Lars explained. "And if that's the case, it's *very* serious."

"How serious?" I asked, my stomach sinking.

"Betrayal," Massimo said. "The end of a 20-year alliance... potentially all-out war."

I'd thought it couldn't get any worse than an attempt on our lives –

But from the way Valentino, Massimo, and Lars were acting, apparently it could.

When our limousine arrived back at the house, there were a dozen armed men out front.

All the remaining brothers were waiting for us – Dario, Niccolo, Adriano, and Roberto.

One of the armed men opened the limousine door for me.

As soon as I stepped out, Dario was right there.

He gently touched my cheek and asked, "Are you alright?"

The tenderness and concern in his voice...

...it was so unlike him.

Suddenly the entire experience hit me again.

The sound of gunshots and breaking glass –

The terror of thinking I was about to die.

My eyes welled up, and I nodded.

Dario drew me to him and wrapped his arms around me.

"You're safe now," he murmured in my ear. "You're safe."

Adriano helped Massimo out of the back of the limousine. Lars tried to help him back to the house, but Massimo brushed him off.

"Fuck you," he said with good humor. "I'm not a 98-year-old grandma."

"Yeah, I don't know any 98-year-old grandmas that weigh 280 pounds," Lars replied.

Dario left my side just long enough to hug both Valentino and Massimo. "I'm glad you're both alright."

Massimo brushed it off. "Meh... I've had stubbed toes worse than this."

"He saved my life," I said.

Everyone turned to look at me.

I blushed at being the center of attention... but I kept going.

"They both did," I continued. "Valentino ran to get the car, but Massimo put himself between me and the gunmen. He's the only reason I'm still alive."

"Then I have twice as much to thank you for," Dario said as he patted Massimo's cheek.

"It was nothing," the big man said shyly.

Valentino coughed humorously to lighten the mood. "I'd say getting the car was absolutely crucial."

"Don't forget running like a frightened squirrel," Massimo replied.

"That, too," Valentino agreed.

Dario clapped Valentino on the shoulder. "Excellent work."

Valentino acted like he was brushing off the compliment... then grinned. "I know."

Dario came back and put his arm around me.

I was shocked at his open show of affection for me in front of his brothers...

...but I welcomed it all the same.

"Well, *consigliere?*" Massimo said. "You're uncharacteristically silent."

"That's because Dario thinks we may be at war," Niccolo said.

"Yeah," Massimo sighed, "that's what we figured."

"What happened in the meeting?" Valentino asked.

"Let's go inside to trade stories," Niccolo said. "There's a lot to talk about."

As he led the way back inside the house, Dario kept his arm around my waist and never let go.

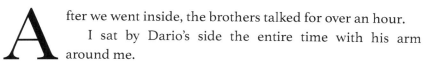fter we went inside, the brothers talked for over an hour.

I sat by Dario's side the entire time with his arm around me.

It was the only way I felt safe.

I barely even listened to their talk of the Agrellas and some mysterious figure they referred to as the Turk.

"Bastard has a scar from his ear all the way down to his mouth," Adriano said. "Looks like he was on the losing end of a knife fight."

"Let's make sure he's on the losing end of *this* fight, too," Niccolo said.

At one point Roberto looked over at me warily and asked, "Should she be here for this?"

"She got shot at, too," Massimo replied. "Anybody who got shot at can stay, as far as I'm concerned."

I was touched by his response.

Nothing else about my presence was brought up for the rest of the evening.

We finally retired to the dining room, where a simple meal of pasta and cold cuts was laid out for us.

However, I was exhausted and not hungry at all.

"I really don't have an appetite," I said. "I think I'm going to go upstairs instead."

"Are you alright?" Dario asked with real concern in his eyes.

"Yes, I'm just... it was a lot."

"Sleep well, Alessandra," Niccolo said, and everyone else in the room repeated it.

Dario watched me go. His eyes were the last thing I saw as I left.

I went to my room, undressed, and put on my negligee.

As soon as I lay down in bed, though, images and sounds from that afternoon came crashing back.

The gunshots –

The screams of the crowd –

The absolute terror I'd felt –

The certainty that I was going to die...

I began to tremble uncontrollably.

Suddenly there was a knock at the door.

"Come in," I called out as I got control of myself.

I figured it was Filomena coming in to check on me –

But it wasn't.

It was Dario.

He walked over and sat on the bed next to me. "Are you alright?"

"...I'm fine," I said as bravely as possible.

He looked at me with his piercing gaze. "Don't bullshit me. Are you alright?"

I tried to keep my composure...

But my face crumpled, the tears came, and I shook my head *no.*

He kicked off his shoes, got into bed beside me, and opened his arms. I snuggled in next to his strong chest as he wrapped me in his embrace.

I immediately began to relax.

I had been so frightened of him when I first saw him at my father's café...

And I'd continued to be afraid of him for the next couple of days.

But now, he was the only thing that made me feel safe.

The only thing that made me feel *protected.*

He held me against him as my tears subsided.

Then he began to speak.

"The first gunfight I was in, I was 15 years old. Men came to the house to kill my father. He sent my mother away with Adriano, Niccolo, Roberto, and Valentino. But he gave me a gun and said, 'This day will come sooner or later. It's time to face it.'"

I reared back and stared at him. "Your father put you in a gunfight when you were *15 years old?!*"

He smiled. "It wasn't just me and my father – it was a dozen of his men, too. And I had been training for *years* for that exact moment. All of us had been... but Adriano was only 13, Niccolo and Roberto were 10, and Valentino was only 7. They were still children."

"You were still a child, too," I insisted.

"Not in this family, I wasn't. My father had been preparing me to take over for him since I was born. That gun battle was the first time I realized how terrifying life could be." Dario gently pushed a strand of my hair away from my face. "All I'm trying to say is that I know it was awful for you today. I'm sorry it happened... and I regret ever putting you in that situation."

"You didn't know... did you?" I asked, suddenly uneasy.

"I had no idea, or I never would have let you leave the house."

I nestled my head against his chest again. "Well... I'm safe now... right?"

"Absolutely," he murmured. "I promise."

He stroked my back as he held me close...

...and suddenly I wanted more.

I lifted my face up to his... stared him in the eyes...

And then kissed him softly on the mouth.

He returned it gently.

We kissed like that for several minutes, slow and romantic...

And then I felt his fingers slide beneath my negligee.

He began stroking my back, bare skin on skin...

And I could feel his cock getting hard inside his pants.

His right hand traced around my side...

And he began to caress my breasts as we kissed.

When his fingers brushed against my hard nipples, a thrill went through my entire body.

Then his hand moved down to my underwear and slipped in the front.

I felt his fingers move through my curls and farther down...

Gently part my lips, which were *so* wet...

And then he used my wetness to lubricate his fingertip as he began to gently circle my clit.

I began to moan, then abruptly stopped myself.

"What's wrong?" he asked with a frown.

"...they can hear me," I whispered in embarrassment.

He gave a devilish smile. "If it bothers you, I'll make them all go stand in the fields every time I take you to bed."

I laughed. "You can't do that!"

"Can't I?" he whispered seductively in my ear as he stroked my clit. "I'm the head of the family. I can make them do whatever I want. And what I *want*... is to hear you come."

His words turned me on even more. I gasped to hear him say it.

I held onto his muscular body as the pleasure rose between my legs –

But I reached down and grabbed his hand to stop him.

"What?" he asked in exasperation. "I'm going to go send them out right now, I swear to God – "

"It's not that," I said shyly. I tugged at his shirt. "I want you to take your clothes off."

"Oh," he said with a laugh – then stood up beside the bed and quickly began to undress.

The moon coming through the window was the only light in the room, but it was enough.

I watched, entranced, as his shirt came off, exposing his muscular chest and perfect abs...

The tattoos covering his olive skin...

And then his pants slipped off, revealing his manhood, long and thick and hard.

I put out a longing hand to touch it.

He smiled as my tiny hand closed around his cock and slowly moved down the length of his shaft.

"You need to take this off, too," he said, grabbing my negligee and lifting it over my head.

Then he pulled at my panties. I raised my ass off the bed so he could more easily peel them off my body.

Then he laid down next to me, the entire length of his muscular body against mine. His hard cock pressed against my belly as he began to kiss me again.

We did that for another few minutes, and then his hand began to move down between my legs.

"Dario," I whispered.

"Yes?"

I looked at him shyly.

"What?" he prodded.

"I... I want you. Inside me."

He smiled. "Let me get you ready first."

"What do you mean, get me... ohhhh..."

I began to moan as he kissed his way down my neck to my breasts...

Where he gently sucked my nipples.

Then he continued to my belly, where he left soft kisses...

On his way to my pussy, where he began to lick.

"Oh, Dario," I whispered.

My eyes closed as his tongue caressed my clit.

Then I felt something part my lips and gently move inside me.

I gasped.

It took me a second to realize it was his finger.

Then he began to move it inside me...

Curling it...

Stroking inside me...

All while licking my clit.

The feeling was amazing.

It added to the intensity of his tongue on my pussy –

But it made me hunger for more.

I wanted to be completely filled up.

But it felt too good...

All I could do was lie there with my eyes rolled back in my head.

The pleasure inside me was building – higher and higher –

When suddenly his finger withdrew.

I was about to ask *Why did you STOP?!* in a disappointed voice –

When an even greater pressure eased back inside me.

Two fingers.

He began to stroke me again as he licked.

I groaned with pleasure.

The feeling of being filled up was even greater –

And I *loved* it.

But it made me want his cock even more.

I writhed on the sheets, my body responding to both his tongue and fingers.

"Dario," I gasped.

"Mm?" he murmured.

To be fair, he couldn't say much more since his mouth was otherwise engaged.

"I'm going to scream," I whispered in panic. "It feels too good!"

His free hand gestured towards me like *Come on, do it.*

"But they'll hear!" I moaned.

I was getting too close –

I wasn't going to be able to control myself –

And then Dario reached out, grabbed the nearest pillow, and threw it at my chest.

The message was clear.

I clamped it over my face and screamed into it as I came.

My entire body tensed as waves of pleasure rolled through me, radiating out from my clit and where he was stroking inside me –

And I continued to scream until I was hoarse.

Finally the waves of pleasure began to recede.

I felt him stop licking and stroking me, and then his body slid across mine as he plucked the pillow away.

He grinned when he saw my face. I'm sure I looked like I was in a drunken stupor.

"I think we solved the problem about them hearing you scream," he whispered.

"...good..." I mumbled.

"Do you still want me inside you?"

Suddenly I was wide awake, and my heart skipped a beat.

"...yes," I whispered.

He kissed me on the lips, and I could taste my own body on his mouth.

I liked it.

I liked knowing he'd been tasting me the whole time he gave me so much pleasure.

"Alright," he murmured. "But we'll take it slow."

## 33

H e lay on his side so I had full access to the front of his body.

We started out by kissing slow and romantic.

The entire time, he fondled my breasts...

And I softly moved my fingers up and down the length of his cock.

He got so turned on that a single drop of wetness dribbled from the slit in his swollen head.

I ran my fingers through the liquid and caressed his cock with it.

It made everything so slippery that I could go faster... my skin gliding over his...

He grunted with pleasure.

His cock had a single contraction... then another...

Tiny spasms that made him bigger for just a second...

And which produced even *more* of his slippery wetness.

"Are you ready?" he finally whispered.

I nodded shyly and slowly spread my legs for him.

He moved on top of me and grasped his shaft in his hand.

He kissed me on the lips, then smiled. "Just the tip at first."

I bit my lip and looked down as he placed his swollen head against my pussy.

I couldn't see what was going on –

But I felt it.

Oh my God –

It was *bliss.*

Soft and huge and firm, the wet crown of his head met *my* wetness and slowly eased inside me.

I gasped.

"Too much?" he asked.

I shook my head rapidly. "No!"

He chuckled... then eased forward just a little bit more.

"Oh!" I cried out.

He pulled out immediately.

"No, wait, don't go!" I whined.

"I thought I was hurting you," he murmured as he kissed my ear, then my mouth.

"Maybe a little," I admitted. Then I added in a voice thick with desire, "But it felt *so good.*"

He smiled again.

This time he stayed right above me, propped up on one elbow.

And with his other hand, he guided himself back to my pussy...

And slooooowly eased himself inside.

He stared deep into my eyes as he did it...

And I felt I was joined with him on an almost spiritual level as his body became one with mine.

My mouth made an 'O' of surprise as he eased a tiny bit deeper inside me.

"Breathe," he commanded.

I took a couple of deep breaths.

"Just get used to it," he whispered.

I nodded, unable to speak.

Then I felt his finger touch my clit again.

The feeling of his cock in my pussy –

And the knowledge that *Oh my god, he's inside me!* –

Plus that gentle, soft caress on my clit?

I immediately came.

I cried out as pleasure rolled up through my belly and into my chest. My nipples tingled with the sensation.

"Ah," Dario whispered with a smile. "So *that's* the secret."

He kissed me again, then stared deep into my eyes as he gently circled my clit...

And eased slooooowly deeper inside me.

I hung onto his gaze like a drowning woman –

A woman drowning in pleasure, that is.

It was like my entire body was one giant wave of orgasmic bliss.

I could feel him sinking deeper and deeper inside me...

His naked cock inside my pussy...

His shaft thick and hot...

And I just kept coming and coming, harder and harder.

The more he filled me up, the deeper inside me he was, the harder I came.

I kept staring into his eyes, and he into mine.

I grabbed onto his broad shoulders and dug my fingernails into his skin –

And I continued to come, wave after wave, not knowing where one orgasm ended and another one began.

He eventually stopped touching my clit and just lay there on top of me, bracing his weight on his forearms as he gazed into my eyes.

The orgasms slowly receded, although I felt like my body was still floating on an ocean of pleasure. Gentle swells, though, not the crashing waves that had been moving *through* me just a minute ago.

He smiled. "Everything okay?"

I nodded vigorously. "Everything is *wonderful.*"

He laughed, then kissed me.

Suddenly there was a contraction in his cock.

I felt it get the tiniest bit bigger inside me.

"Oh!" I cried out, loving the feeling.

He grinned. "Felt that, did you?"

"Oh yes..."

"Mmm... how about this?" he asked as he slowly pulled a few inches out of me...

...and then just as slowly eased his cock back in.

My eyes rolled back in my head.

*"Madonn,"* I moaned.

He laughed out loud.

I laughed along with him, though I blushed.

"That's the first time I've ever heard you curse," he whispered.

"You make me do all sorts of things I never thought I would."

"Mmmm... well, let's see if we can make you do a few more."

He kissed me, his tongue moving softly over mine...

Then he began to rock his hips back and forth, slowly withdrawing from me and easing back inside.

I groaned with pleasure. It was a different feeling than when he caressed my clit, but it was such a *satisfying* feeling...

Him completely filling me up...

Our bodies joined in overwhelming pleasure.

I could feel all sorts of little things...

Like how the ridge on his crown moved over the spot inside me, the same place he had caressed with his fingers...

The way the head of his cock touched pleasurable places inside me that I never even knew existed...

The way I could feel him getting thicker inside me as he went from halfway in to *all* the way down to the base of his shaft.

Then he began to move slightly faster.

The gentle pleasure I'd felt with his slow movements began to grow *much* more intense.

I gasped as he began to thrust inside me.

Fast strokes followed by a couple of slow ones...

Then another thrust went *deep* inside me. A tiny throb of pain mixed in with the overwhelming pleasure.

I heard the wet sound of his body against mine, *slap slap slap!*

I could feel his balls dangling against my ass, a tickle in a place I didn't expect it –

And then all of that seemed to go away as I had an orgasm unlike all the others I had experienced.

It came from *deep* within me, a contraction and release of pure pleasure that went from the top of my head down to my toes.

I was totally lost in pleasure, drowning in it –

And I screamed as I came harder and harder.

Suddenly Dario was bellowing in my ear –

And then he was coming, too.

I could feel something hot and wet spurt deep inside me as his cock throbbed over and over in tiny spasms.

The knowledge that *he* was coming – that I had *made* him come inside me – pushed me even higher.

I gave one long, final shriek of ecstasy as my orgasm reached its peak.

His thrusts began to slow down...

And my own wave of pleasure began to recede, though little tremors of bliss still rushed through me.

I could feel the occasional single spasm of his cock inside me.

He eventually stopped moving.

His cock was still hard inside me, though perhaps not quite as big as before.

He kissed me gently, sweetly.

We stayed like that for another few moments...

Him still inside me, kissing me...

Until he finally withdrew.

# 34

---

We lay in each other's arms afterwards. I snuggled against him, and his fingers softly brushed across my bare skin.

"How was your first time?" he asked.

"Heaven," I murmured.

He chuckled. "Good. But how are you feeling *now?*"

"Wonderful. But... a little sore."

I *was* sore, it was true... but it was a delicious soreness because it was the memory of him inside me.

I let my hand drift over his abs... down to his thatch of hair... and caressed his heavy, limp cock. Even soft, it felt enormous in my hand.

At my touch, it began to stir back to life, expanding slowly in length with each of his heartbeats.

"Careful," he said humorously. "Don't wake the dragon."

"The monster..." I added playfully...

Then froze.

The words made me think of the first night I had seen him – because that was what I had called him in my head:

*Il Mostro.*

Suddenly I remembered how he had bent down and whispered in my ear, *You will be my whore. But only for me... and no one else.*

Dario felt me tense up. "What is it?"

"...nothing."

He pushed me gently onto my back and looked deep into my eyes.

"What?" he demanded.

A tear welled up at the edge of my eye and slowly traced its way down my face.

"I guess I'm your whore now," I said bitterly as I turned away from him.

He put his hand on my chin and forced me to look at him.

"You... are my *woman* now," he whispered. "And only for me... and no one else."

A sob escaped my chest, and I smiled through my tears.

He leaned over to kiss me...

And I kissed him back passionately...

And we made love again.

# 35

We slept in each other's arms throughout the night.

As the sun dawned through the glass doors of my room, my eyes opened the tiniest bit.

I smiled as I felt his body behind mine, spooning me...

His muscles pressed against my feminine softness...

And then suddenly my eyes opened wide.

"Wake up!" I whispered frantically as I turned around and began to shake him.

Dario was instantly awake. He sat up in bed and looked around the room for some kind of threat. "What?! What is it?!"

"You have to leave!"

He looked at me, confused. "...what? Why?"

"Because they'll know you spent the night!"

He smirked. "I'm pretty sure everyone already knows it."

I stared at him. "...why?"

"Well, you only used the pillow over your face the *first* time you came."

I thought back to the night before and realized he was right.

I'd been so overcome with making love to him – so overwhelmed by pleasure – that I'd forgotten everything else.

I covered my face with my hands and moaned into them. "Oh my god..."

He laughed and lay back down next to me.

I suddenly felt his hand on my breast.

"We can wake them up, too..." he murmured seductively in my ear.

"Are you insane?!" I hissed, slapping his hand away. "You have to go! NOW!"

He looked at me like I was crazy. "What's gotten into you?"

"If you don't go *now*, Filomena will know you were here!"

He squinted in bewilderment. "...Filomena...?"

"The old lady servant!" When he didn't react, I exclaimed, "You don't know her?!"

"She must have been hired while I was in prison." Dario yawned, then reached around me and pulled my naked body next to his. "I'll be damned if I'm going to let some old woman interfere with – "

"GO!" I whispered loudly as I pushed him out of bed.

He shook his head in amused wonder. "I'm the head of the most powerful family in Tuscany, and I'm getting kicked out of bed because of some old grandmother."

"Go, go!" I said, shooing him away.

He sighed and picked up his clothes from the floor. "Only for you."

I smiled...

And admired his nude body as he leaned over to pick up his pants...

And thought for a second that *maaaaybe* I should have him stay...

But then he started walking towards the door.

Naked.

"What are you DOING?!" I hissed.

"Leaving," he said crossly.

"You can't go out like *that!*"

"No one's awake, Alessandra."

"But if she is and she *sees* you – !"

"Then maybe she'll have a heart attack and die, and I won't have to be kicked out of your bed again."

But he stepped into his pants and pulled them on.

I breathed a sigh of relief.

"You realize that she'll still know *exactly* what happened if I walk out of your room at 6 in the morning," he said.

"Better *that* than for her to see all the goods!" I whispered.

He chuckled as he put on his shirt. "By the way, the meeting with my uncle is at 10AM."

My heart fell a little. "Alright... I'll stay in my room..."

"No – I'm telling you because I want you to be there."

I stared at him in wonder. "Why?"

"You were shot at just like Massimo and Valentino. You might have seen something they've forgotten."

"...oh..."

At that moment, I felt included in a way I never had before.

He winked and smiled. "Plus you're my woman now."

My heart skipped a beat –

But he was out the door and gone before I could reply.

I lay back down in bed with a happy smile.

I felt a pleasant soreness between my thighs that reminded me of what we had done last night...

And began to regret kicking him out.

# 36

As soon as word came that Fausto was on the property, all of us – Dario, me, his brothers, and Lars – went out onto the front steps of the mansion.

A small fleet of black Mercedes and BMWs drove up. In the middle was a silver Rolls Royce. The cars parked, and a dozen men in suits got out. They were mostly in their 30s and 40s – unlike Dario's men, who were almost all in their 20s.

Niccolo read my mind. "When our uncle split off from the family, most of our former staff went with him," he explained.

"Which is apparently why we had to hire bothersome old maids as servants," Dario muttered under his breath.

"What?" Niccolo said. "I didn't catch that – "

"Nothing," I said as I kicked the side of Dario's shoe with my foot. He just smirked in silence.

The doors of the Rolls Royce opened and two men got out.

One was youthful, maybe five years older than me. He was tall, wiry, and less powerful-looking than Dario. He wore his long, black hair in a ponytail down the back of his neck. His face was cruel, and his eyes were so dark that they seemed almost black.

I shivered when he glanced at me and was glad when he looked away.

The other man was much older – in his 50s, probably. He was powerfully built but with a slight gut that his expensive three-piece suit couldn't hide. He had a mustache and goatee, and his eyes twinkled mischievously beneath heavy brows. His black hair was grey at the temples, and some of it also streaked his beard.

"Don Rosolini," he said in a playful voice as he walked towards Dario.

"Uncle Fausto," Dario said as he embraced him. "Thank you for coming."

"My pleasure. Niccolo, Adriano, Roberto – excellent to see you. Valentino, still too damn pretty for your own good." Fausto turned to Massimo. "You holding up alright?"

"I am – thank you, *padrone,*" Massimo said warmly.

"Good. I'm glad you took down a few of the bastards yourself."

Then Fausto turned to me.

"This is Alessandra," Niccolo said.

"Ahhh... so *this* is the little girl who's caused so much trouble."

I turned to Dario in surprise.

It was Niccolo who answered, though. "Your father's café is technically in Uncle Fausto's territory. We had to notify him of our intentions the night we dealt with the intruder."

"And deal with him you did," Fausto said. He clapped Lars on the shoulder. "If you ever get tired of working for my nephews, come and see me. I could always use a man like you."

Lars just smiled politely.

The man with the ponytail walked up.

"May I introduce my son Aurelio," Fausto said to me.

"Like Marcus Aurelius?" I asked, mentioning the Roman Emperor from almost 2000 years ago.

"Exactly."

Aurelio said nothing. He just watched me with that cold, unsettling gaze of his.

"Shall we go inside?" Niccolo said, then led the way.

Dario offered his arm to me.

I smiled as I took it, and he escorted me inside.

I couldn't help but notice that Aurelio never took his eyes off me.

## 37

When we sat down in the parlor, the daggers finally came out.

"You vouched for the Turk," Dario said coldly. "I turned down his business proposal. Not an hour later, Massimo, Valentino, and Alessandra were attacked."

"Regrettable, truly," Fausto said. He sounded pained as he said it.

"Why did you send a viper into my home?" Dario asked, his voice angry but controlled.

"I'm not so sure that *he* is the viper you're searching for," Fausto said. "And I would caution you against assuming it was the Turk who ordered the hit."

"You're saying it was the Agrellas?"

"I didn't say that, either."

"The Turk is *working* with the Agrellas," Dario said. "You don't think it's an extraordinary coincidence that the attack took place in their territory?"

"Someone certainly *wants* you to believe the Agrellas and the Turk are behind this."

"But you don't believe they are," Dario said contemptuously.

"No."

"And why is that?"

"Because *we're* working with him, too," Aurelio spoke up.

Everyone in the room looked at him in surprise – then turned back to Fausto.

Fausto gave his son a reproachful look, then sighed. "Yes, it's true – we're in business with him."

Dario stared at him. "Why didn't you tell me this before yesterday's meeting?"

"Because I didn't want you to feel pressured by my decision."

Dario narrowed his eyes. "I *wouldn't* have. Believe me."

"Mm," Fausto murmured noncommittally.

"What exactly are the terms of your deal?" Roberto asked.

"Always the head for business, this one," Fausto said with a chuckle. "The Turk wants to sell some of his wares in our territory, and he offered a healthy cut of the profits. I said yes."

Dario glared at his uncle. "Sex trafficking and drugs."

Fausto made a face like *What can I do?* "Business is business."

"Not everyone is as squeamish as you, cousin," Aurelio smirked.

Dario glared at Aurelio. "And not everyone will whore themselves out for a dollar like *you*... cousin."

Aurelio's face showed barely restrained fury.

There was an instant crackle of tension in the room.

Adriano, Lars, and Massimo all leaned forward in their chairs.

Fausto's men inched their hands towards the insides of their jackets.

"Boys," Fausto said loudly as he gave Aurelio an angry look.

"I'm not your *boy*," Dario snarled.

"No, but you're very new to your position," Fausto replied. "Your father wouldn't have said 'no' to the Turk."

"I'm not my father."

"That much is apparent," Aurelio muttered.

Before Dario could respond with another insult, Niccolo jumped in. "We've made the decision not to deal in certain things going forward. That's all."

"What, you're a bunch of angels, now?" Fausto said contemptuously. "Last I checked, the authorities would hang you for all the *other* crimes you dabble in."

"Yes, well, that's why we own the authorities," Dario said with a cold smile.

"Which is why I sent you the Turk. You need to shore up your territory if you want to survive. You can offer him access to the police and judges, and he can give you a steady stream of revenue. It's a win-win proposition."

Niccolo shook his head. "The police and judges are willing to look away when it comes to gambling and stolen goods. They won't ignore trafficking women and drugs."

"So throw them some more money," Fausto said with a shrug.

"Let me be clear, Uncle," Dario said. "*I refuse to deal with traf-ficking women and drugs.*"

"You should go into the priesthood, then," Fausto replied. "Maybe you could become pope. You do the 'sanctimonious' part extremely well."

"Gentlemen," Niccolo said, "this has nothing to do with the most pressing matter at hand. Members of our family were shot at yester-day. We *must* retaliate."

"Or you'll look weak," Fausto said with a benevolent smile.

"Exactly."

The older man's smile disappeared. "You already look weak. The whole of the *Cosa Nostra* knows you're struggling. The wolves are sali-vating over what they'll do to you. Your territory is divided – "

"Half of which went to *you,*" Dario pointed out.

"Which is why I made a deal with the Turk," Fausto shot back. "How long can you sustain your current operations?"

"We're fine," Roberto said. "Better than fine, actually. We plan to expand globally into online gambling. In fact, we could be fully legit-imate within two years."

That was the first I had heard of the family's long-term plans.

I looked at Dario in surprise.

He smiled the tiniest bit and nodded almost imperceptibly.

Fausto wasn't convinced, though.

"You've been going on and on about this online gambling nonsense for five years," he said in a bored voice. "Talk, talk, talk."

"Because Father never let me pursue it," Roberto said in irritation. "But Dario *is*."

"Lovely," Fausto sneered, "but you yourself said it could take two years. You still have a significant number of bribes to pay every month – a lot of judges and police captains looking to wet their beaks. Where's *that* money coming from?"

"It's covered," Roberto said, although he didn't sound entirely convincing.

"Don't bullshit me," Fausto snapped. "I was your father's *consigliere* for 20 years – I know the financials of this entire operation like the back of my hand. I *know* you have maybe six months left at your current levels of income. I sent you the Turk so you can prosper and grow. As of right now, you're withering on the vine."

Dario's voice was full of contempt. "So we should bend the knee to some foreign bastard who insults me in my own home? Just because dear old Uncle Fausto knows best?"

"Again," Niccolo said sharply, "back to the matter at hand. If we're going to send a message, we need to know who to send it to."

"It wasn't the Agrellas or the Turk," Fausto said with a sniff.

"And how do you know *that*?" Dario asked mockingly. "Did you ask them?"

"Did you ever find out about the Genoan?" Fausto pointed at Lars and me. "The one your Swede killed in her father's café?"

Niccolo clenched his jaws. "We're still working on it."

"Why is she even *here*?" Aurelio snarled as he looked at me. Then he smirked at Dario. "Is she your whore now? Maybe you thought you might want a blowjob halfway through the meeting."

I flinched at his ugly words.

Dario put his hand on mine before he answered.

"She survived a gunfight in the streets yesterday," Dario said coldly. "Which is more than *you've* ever done, little *boy*."

Aurelio immediately stood up, furious –

And every Rosolini brother bolted to their feet as well.

Lars even had his hand inside his jacket.

I was terrified, sure that there would be another gun battle –

"STOP!" Fausto roared. "Aurelio, sit DOWN, goddamn you! We're family, so fucking act like it!"

Aurelio's face twitched with rage, but he sat back down.

Lars and all the Rosolini brothers did as well – but slowly.

"I talked to Stefano Agrella," Fausto said. "He swore on his mother's grave that he had nothing to do with the hit yesterday."

"So of *course* you believe him," Dario replied sarcastically.

"I've done business with the Agrellas for 20 years. I'd know if Stefano was fucking me. He's not."

"What about the Turk?"

"I talked to him as well. He says he's not involved, and I believe him."

"You're taking his money," Adriano sneered. "It's in your best *interests* to believe him."

Fausto shot daggers at Adriano. "And it's in *your* best interest not to open your mouth since you don't know what the fuck you're talking about."

Before Adriano could respond, Fausto turned back to Dario. "The Turk is doing business with me, so what possible reason would he have to enrage *you*? If he killed Massimo or Valentino – my *own blood* – he knows I would break off all business dealings with him. Not only *that,* but I'd join you and go to war against him. The Turk is a businessman, first and foremost. There's no profit in war – he knows that."

"Unless he could take our territory for himself," Niccolo said.

"If he was going to kill you," Fausto replied, "he would have murdered *all* of you at the same time. Not just pick off two of you in Florence, enrage the rest of you, and start a war."

All of the brothers were silent.

Even *I* had to admit that what their uncle said made sense.

Fausto shook his head. "Someone *wants* you to think the Turk and the Agrellas are trying to kill you. Someone *wants* to blow up the situation. Find out who that is, and you'll find out who tried to kill Massimo and Valentino yesterday."

"And Alessandra," Dario said.

"...and Alessandra," Fausto agreed. He smiled at me... and a shiver ran down my spine.

# 38

Dario

After the meeting, everyone was supposed to have lunch together – but no one could be bothered to keep up the charade of 'one big happy family.'

Fausto said his goodbyes and promised to pass on any information that came his way. Aurelio just ignored us and got back in the Rolls Royce with his father.

As they drove away, Alessandra looked at me with wide eyes. "Was that... normal?"

I smiled grimly. "Things were different when my father was alive."

"Although Aurelio was *always* a little prick," Adriano said.

"More like a gigantic asshole who *has* a little prick," Valentino muttered.

As we made our way to the patio for lunch, Niccolo asked Alessandra, "What did *you* think?"

"I don't trust either of them." She suddenly looked nervous, like she was afraid she shouldn't have said it out loud. "...not to insult your uncle or cousin..."

"Insult away," I said. "They did their fair share of insulting *us.*"

"*Why* don't you trust them?" Niccolo asked her.

"Well... I've seen a lot of people pass through my father's café. Most have been pleasant, but there are always difficult customers. Aurelio reminds me of the ones who are never satisfied. They walk in the door angry, and nothing you can say or do will win them over. They're *looking* for a fight. And Fausto is like the overly friendly man who acts like your best friend to your face, but then you find all the packets of sugar and honey are missing after he's gone. And he usually shortchanges you on the bill, as well."

Niccolo burst out laughing, then turned to me. "I don't think she could have described *either* of them more perfectly."

"True," I agreed.

Alessandra blushed and smiled at the praise.

"I want to discuss something with Dario for a moment," Niccolo told her. "Go join the others for lunch, and we'll be there in just a moment."

She nodded, gave me a smile, and walked off towards the patio.

"What is it?" I asked.

"News came in about that priest and the lowlife at the church," Niccolo said. "I literally got a text at the end of the meeting."

"And?"

"Connections to the Oldani family," Niccolo said.

The Oldanis were the most powerful crime family in Genoa, 150 miles from Florence. They had also employed Umberto Fumagalli, the man Lars had gunned down in Alessandra's café.

"The timing's suspicious," I muttered, "coming right after Fausto's speech about 'find out who's behind it all.'"

"Normally I would say yes, but the tip came from an old friend who wormed his way into Interpol," Niccolo said. "Not even Fausto knows about him."

"So the Genoans are after our territory..."

"The first wolves to show up after Papa's death, it seems."

"It still doesn't explain why their lieutenant was at the café that night. Have you spoken to Alessandra's father since then?"

Niccolo nodded. "I've called the café twice. He still swears he knows nothing."

"So either it really *was* a coincidence..."

"...or the old man's holding out," Niccolo finished. "And his secrets are worse than letting his daughter be held captive."

I shook my head. "What a mess."

"You should have gotten the truth out of him before you started sleeping with his daughter. Now you're emotionally involved."

I scowled at him. "Watch yourself, *consigliere.*"

"I don't want to say 'I told you so' – but *I told you so*. I don't think we'll be beating the truth out of him now." Niccolo smirked. "After all, Alessandra might object."

I just glared at him as we joined the others for lunch.

## 39

Alessandra

Dario came to me again that night.

By the time he arrived, I was craving him...

Hungering for his touch.

He walked over to the bed where I lay, my heart pounding...

And he bent over, took me in his arms, and kissed me hungrily.

Then he stood up from the bed and ripped off his jacket and shirt.

I watched, entranced, as he revealed his washboard abs... the tattoos covering his chest and shoulders...

But when he began to unbuckle his pants, I couldn't help myself.

I reached out –

Then realized what I had just done and pulled back my hand shyly.

Dario smiled. "Go ahead."

I sat up on the edge of the bed and slowly pulled his belt out of its loops.

Then, innocently gazing up at him, I unzipped his pants and let them fall around his thighs.

His cock was already jutting up from under his black boxers.

I touched it through the cloth, cupped its thickness in my hand...

And then, licking my lips, I slowly tugged down his underwear.

I had to pull the cloth out far from his body to let his cock spring free.

When it did, it jolted up in the air with a bounce, stiff and hard.

I stared at it, fascinated and lustful...

And slowly took it in my hand.

The skin was feverishly hot but velvety soft.

I looked up at his face.

"Go ahead," he murmured. "Do whatever you want."

I held the thick base of his cock in my hand...

And then I leaned forward and kissed it.

Maybe it was stupid or too innocent.

I didn't know what to do to please him...

But what I *did* know was I wanted to feel my lips on his cock.

I kissed his swollen head...

Then the underside of his shaft...

And then the side...

Tiny, soft kisses with my eyes closed...

Feeling his scorching heat on my lips...

Smelling his manly scent.

Then I licked him.

Just a tiny, soft, wet stroke of my tongue.

I loved his taste: clean skin and the tiniest bit of salt.

My tongue traced down the side of his cock...

And then I licked him some more underneath.

He threw his head back and groaned...

...so I guess he liked it.

I know *I* liked it.

I began to lick him up and down like an ice cream cone.

His cock spasmed in my hand, and a dew drop of liquid appeared at the slit in his crown.

I licked that, and it was even saltier.

I put my lips slowly over his tip and got his swollen head all the way in my mouth.

He was *big*.

It was a lot...

But I loved having him in my mouth.

I felt him pulse bigger for a second, then tasted a bit more saltiness.

I took his cock out of my mouth and began to lick it again –

And then he lost control.

He stepped backwards, roughly yanked my negligee up over my head, and then picked me up and tossed me onto the bed.

I cried out in happy surprise.

I liked the feel of him moving me wherever he wanted...

And then he did much, *much* more.

He quickly shucked off his pants. Then he pried open my legs and was on top of me, kissing my mouth, cupping my breast in his hand.

I was already soaking wet with anticipation.

His cock was already wet from my mouth, so he quickly slid inside me.

I cried out as he entered. He filled me up so rapidly that it took my breath away.

At first it hurt the tiniest bit –

But it felt *so good* the deeper he got...

The thicker his cock became as he sank into me...

That I grabbed his muscular ass and pulled him deeper inside me.

He grunted like an animal and began to thrust.

I cried out as he rocked in and out of me, taking me higher and higher.

He reached one hand underneath me and cupped my ass in his palm –

Then began to caress me where not even *he* had touched me before.

The sensation of him stroking my ass...

While his cock went deeper...

His girth filling me up...

It was too much.

My first orgasm exploded deep inside me.

I cried out and hung onto his neck as he continued to rock inside me...

Every movement varying from shallow to deep.

He surprised me with every thrust. I could never guess how deeply he would go.

He kissed my mouth, my ears, my neck – bit me gently –

Fondled my breasts and stroked my nipples –

And all the time he was rocking in and out of me, making me lose control.

My second orgasm came just a minute after the first.

I wrapped my legs around his waist and hung on to him for dear life.

Time seemed to slow down and then stop completely.

All I know is that waves of pleasure overlapped one another.

One orgasm would trail off...

Then entirely *new* contractions would send shivers from my head to my toes.

Finally Dario grunted and bellowed –

And I felt him come.

It was indescribably hot: the feeling of his cock exploding inside me –

Liquid heat spurting deep within me –

His weight bearing down on me as he thrust savagely like an animal –

Until gradually he slowed down and stopped moving at all.

I held him close with an enormous smile on my face, just enjoying the feel of his body on mine and his still-hard cock deep inside me.

Then he lifted his head and kissed me.

Softly at first...

Then more hungrily...

And without ever getting soft, he began to rock inside me...

And we did it all over again.

## 40

W e spent the next few nights together like that.

Dario would come to me after everyone else had gone to bed –

And we would make mad, passionate love.

It would last for an hour or more...

Then we would talk...

And do it again. Sometimes twice.

Afterwards, we would fall asleep in each other's arms until dawn – at which point I would make him leave before the rest of the house awoke.

I had begun to accept the situation. I looked forward to his visits every night – and my body hungered for his.

Gradually I stopped feeling guilty for what I was doing...

Until Filomena brought it all crashing down.

I hadn't seen the old woman for days. It was like she was avoiding me.

At first, that bothered me... but I was so enraptured with Dario that I forgot about everything else.

Then I came back to my room after breakfast one morning and found her stripping the sheets off the bed.

The cold hand of fear clutched my heart when I saw her, but I forced myself to say good morning.

She didn't answer, nor did she look at me.

"I haven't seen you the last few days," I said.

She still didn't answer.

Rather than force her to talk to me, I turned back towards the door. "Well, I'll just let you finish what you're doing – "

"Why?" the old woman asked quietly.

I glanced back at her, but she still wouldn't look at me.

"Well, you're busy – "

"That's not what I meant, and you know it," she said. When she finally turned to look at me, there was immense disappointment in her eyes. "What would your sainted mother say, God rest her soul?"

I trembled as I asked, "About what?"

"About you becoming a *mafioso's* whore."

I was shocked into silence.

"Or your father?" the old woman continued. "How ashamed would he be if he knew?"

I couldn't stop the memory of my father pleading with Dario:

*Don Rosolini... Alessandra is a good girl... she goes to mass every Sunday... she's a virgin, padrone...*

"Do you think he wants you spreading your legs like a slut?" she asked.

"You don't get to speak to me like that," I snapped, my voice shaking.

"*Someone* has to. You've forsaken all common sense – given your-self to a murderer who will throw you away like a used tissue when he's finished with you."

"He won't – "

"He *will*. He will, child, he will," she said, and her face suddenly looked pained. "I know you don't want to believe it. You're young, you're innocent, you're in love..."

I flinched.

I hadn't ever said it – I hadn't even allowed myself to *think* it –

But it was true.

I *was* in love with Dario.

Which was why Filomena's next words cut like a knife.

"But you don't know men like I do," she whispered. "Especially not *these* men. They take what they want and they don't care who they hurt. They certainly don't care about a young woman's virtue or what they might do to her heart."

My father's words echoed in my brain:

*Sir, your reputation precedes you... you are a worldly man... and you reap where you do not sow. My daughter is an innocent...*

Filomena's voice grew ominous. "Or what they might do to her *soul*."

"N-nothing's happened," I said.

It was the most unconvincing lie I'd ever told.

She laughed bitterly. "I change your sheets every morning. You think I can't tell you rutted in them like animals the night before? And I know who the animal is. He guards his territory like a wolf; none of the other monsters in this house would dare cross him. That's how vicious he is."

She walked over to me and grabbed my hands, imploring me. "Child... he doesn't care about you. He'll use you for a moment's pleasure, and when his interest fades, he'll cast you out... or worse."

"Get out," I said as I jerked my hands away. My whole body was shaking. "Get *out*."

She looked at me with eyes full of pain. "You can complain about me to your lover, which will probably get me killed. At the very least, banished and left to die penniless. I don't care. I was a mother once. You are like the daughter I never had, and it is because of the love I have for you in my heart that I tell you – "

"Shut up," I whispered, terrified of what she would say next.

"He will never marry you," she said softly. "I'm sorry, but it's true. You will be nothing more to him than a whore. When he's finished with you, he will throw you away... and he will laugh that you gave yourself so easily to him."

Without another word, she turned and walked out of the room.

# 41

Filomena's words haunted me.

I tried to forget what she'd said –

But memories came rushing back, all of them tinged with violence and sin.

Dario showing up in my father's café with his enemy's blood still pooled on the floor.

How he had beaten the man outside the church nearly to death with his bare hands.

The way Dario had first 'punished' me, touching me until I came...

Addicting me to him, then leading me farther down the path of sin until I gave my virginity to him...

Until I gave my *heart* to him.

To a *mafioso*... a murderer.

Was he all bad?

No. Definitely not.

There was kindness in him.

He had saved me from my attacker at the church –

But I would have never been in danger if Dario hadn't kidnapped me in the first place.

Were his brothers all bad?

No. There was kindness in them, too.

Massimo had saved my life in Florence –

But would I have been shot at if they weren't a family of criminals?

Violence attracts violence.

Evil attracts evil.

Death attracts death.

There was goodness in them, yes...

But Lucifer is the angel of light, the most beautiful of the heavenly host...

And still the devil.

Everything around Dario was twisted and dark.

And now he had touched me, leaving his fingerprints on my soul.

I imagined my father walking in on me and Dario.

I could see the horror on his face...

And then I heard Dario's mocking voice:

*I gave you my word, old man.*

*I didn't take your daughter's virginity... until she begged me to do it.*

I had been led astray by sin so sweet that I had forgotten everything else...

But Filomena's words had awoken me to the danger I was in.

The danger my *soul* was in.

I knew I had to change the path I was on...

...or be lost forever.

## 42

I was quiet and withdrawn for the rest of the day.

Dario was preoccupied with business. He didn't ask me about my mood – if he even noticed.

But Niccolo did.

"What's wrong?" the *consigliere* asked after pulling me aside.

"Nothing," I mumbled.

"You're not tired of being cooped up, are you? We can't take you out again for a while, not after what happened in Florence."

"I'm fine. I'm just... feeling down, that's all."

"Alright," he said, still looking concerned. "Let me know if you need anything."

Later in the morning, I went to the kitchen to see Caterina. If anyone could cheer me up, it would be her.

"Hey, Grumpy," she said playfully. "Why so blue?"

I didn't want to tell her what Filomena had said, but I *did* want to ask her some things.

"When we first met, you said all Rosolini men were dogs."

She looked at me and put her hands on her hips angrily. "Did Don Rosolini cheat on you?!"

"No!" I said in shock.

"Oh," she said with a confused look. "...then why did you ask?"

"I just wanted to know what you meant."

She laughed. "What do you *think* I meant? All the Rosolini men are dogs. Pretty self-explanatory."

"So everything that's going on with you and Valentino...?"

She shrugged. "It's fun, but come on – I know what it is. There aren't any glass slippers at the end of the story."

Her flippant manner made me feel even worse. "So... me and Dario...?"

"Oh, sweetie..." Caterina reached out and held my hands. "Enjoy it for what it is: banging a really hot, powerful man, and all that goes along with it."

I was repulsed by her words.

"What, like being kept prisoner?" I asked bitterly.

She tilted her head to one side. "You've really fallen for him, haven't you?"

I jerked my hands away from her. "No!"

"Then why are you so upset?"

"I'm *not!*"

"Could've fooled me." She sighed and gave me a half-hearted smile. "Look, the story ends in one of two ways. Either *we* get tired and try to move on, and they let us or they don't – because, let's face it, these are men who don't like being told 'no.'

"Or *they* get tired and move on, no matter how *we* feel about it. And that's that. So... *carpe diem* and all that bullshit. Seize the day. Enjoy what you've got while you've got it."

I stared at her. "What about the future?"

"What about it?"

"What about getting *married?*"

Cat touched my cheek sadly. "When it happens... it won't be to a Rosolini."

## 43

I told a servant to let Niccolo know I wasn't feeling well, and I stayed in my room during dinner. He had the kitchen send up some food.

Thank God Filomena didn't deliver it.

Later that evening, as I was lying in bed, I heard the door open.

The moment I'd been dreading had come.

Dario came to the bed, leaned over me, and tried to kiss me.

I turned my face away so that he kissed my cheek instead.

He roughly grabbed my chin and turned me towards him – then kissed me on the lips.

I struggled to break free. "Stop!"

He let go of me. "What's wrong?"

"I don't want to tonight."

He switched on the light next to my bed and sat next to me. "Are you alright?"

I looked away from him miserably. He was so handsome that it made me want to give in... to do like Caterina had said and throw caution to the wind.

"...no," I murmured.

He caressed my arm. "What's wrong?"

His touch was so sensual... and I wanted him so badly...

"I'm not your whore," I whispered.

He chuckled and leaned in to kiss my neck. "Of course you are."

I pushed him away. "NO, I'm *not!*"

He stood up, furious and bewildered. "*Madonn* – what's gotten into you?!"

I looked up at him with tears in my eyes. "Do I mean *anything* to you?"

His face softened. "Of course you do. A great deal, actually."

"Do you think of the future... with me in it?"

Dario narrowed his eyes. "Are you asking what I *think* you're asking?"

I suddenly felt embarrassed and insecure. "I don't know... what do you *think* I'm asking?"

"It sounds like you're talking about marriage."

I looked up at him helplessly.

Suddenly, without warning, he laughed.

I stared at him in horror...

Then turned away from him with a heaviness in my heart.

"Alessandra, we've known each other for less than two weeks," he said, his voice slightly angry. It got angrier as he spoke. "I've been the head of my family for only three. I'm in the middle of what could be a war between my family, a gangster from Turkey, and various factions of the *Cosa Nostra,* none of whom will actually challenge me to my face. They want to destroy me and my brothers – to take every-thing we have, everything our father and grandfather built. Death is all around me... financial ruin is staring me in the face... and you're asking me, after a week of fucking, whether I intend to *marry* you?"

*After a week of fucking.*

That was all the answer I needed.

"I want to go home," I whispered.

"You *can't* go home," he snapped. "My enemies are out there."

I looked at him, suddenly furious. "You said it yourself – they want to destroy *you.* They want to destroy YOUR family. They don't give a *damn* about me. So let me go."

He sat down on the bed and tried to take my hand. I wouldn't let him.

"Alessandra," he said, trying to sound reasonable, "they nearly *killed* you in Florence – "

"They nearly killed Massimo and Valentino. I was just there by accident."

Dario turned away from me. I could tell he was angry and trying to control his temper.

When he spoke again, he was at least partially composed. "Look... it's dangerous. They will try to get at me *through* you – "

"And that's all you care about, isn't it?"

"I care about YOU, GOD DAMMIT!" he roared as he stood up from the bed.

I shrank down in fear as he angrily paced back and forth.

Then he sat back down next to me. "I care for you. I do."

"But you don't love me," I whispered.

His face hardened. "What are you saying – that *you* love *me?*"

I nodded, and tears spilled down my cheeks. "Even though I was a fool to do so, it seems."

Something happened to his expression, then – something I had never seen on Dario's face before:

He looked like he was in pain.

Like inside, he was breaking.

"I can't let you go," he whispered.

"I'm just a whore," I said bitterly, "good for a week of fucking. You can always get another."

The vulnerability that *had* been there on his face suddenly disappeared, replaced by a cruel mask.

"So be it," he said coldly. "If that's what you want."

"It's *not* what I want!" I cried out.

"THEN WHAT DO YOU WANT?!" he shouted at me.

"I want you to love me," I sobbed. "I want you to *want* to marry me."

He stared at me for what seemed like forever...

And then he said, "That's the one thing I can't give you."

I broke down crying into my hands.

There was a long silence. Then...

"I'll arrange for someone to take you back," he said quietly.

I heard his footsteps across the floor...

I heard the door open and close...

And he was gone.

I collapsed in the bed and wept...

Maybe even harder than the day my mother had died.

## 44

Niccolo came to fetch me. He had the good sense to wait until I was all cried out, though it took nearly an hour for me to stop.

I was already dressed and lying on the bed when I heard a tap at the door. "Come in."

Niccolo entered and stood there. He looked very sad.

"Are you sure?" he asked quietly.

"...yes."

"It's dangerous out there."

"I'll be fine," I whispered.

"Alessandra – "

"I can't stay here, not a minute longer," I said, my voice hitching as the tears threatened to start again. "Not around Dario."

"Let me send you somewhere else – somewhere safe. Switzerland – France – anywhere in Europe you want to go – "

"I want to go home."

He paused for a long moment before he said, "If they come for you... and it's possible they may... there's nothing I can do to save you. Do you understand?"

"Why would they come for me?"

Niccolo threw up his hands. "I don't know. Maybe in retaliation for what happened that night in the café."

"I had nothing to do with that."

"*I* know that, but – "

"You can tell people that Dario brought me here to get information out of me... and you can say that he broke me." I barely stopped a sob from escaping my throat. "And it will be the truth."

"Alessandra..." Niccolo whispered.

"You've been kind to me, and I appreciate that."

"Except for those threats the first night," he reminded me with a playful smile.

I laughed in spite of myself.

"Except for those. But you've been kind to me ever since." Then my expression changed, and tears filled my eyes. "Please... be kind to me once more... and let me go."

Niccolo stood there a long time... and then he nodded.

"Do you have your things packed?"

The clothes Massimo had bought me in Florence had been left on the street when we ran from the gunmen.

I only had a few dresses I'd brought from home. If I took them with me, I would remember everything that had happened here.

Like Dario taking them off me...

And making love to me.

"You can burn them," I said dully. "And all the memories they hold."

Niccolo sighed heavily... then walked over to the bed, gave me a sad smile, and put out his arm.

I smiled sadly back at him... took his arm...

And he walked me out of the room.

# 45

All the brothers were waiting for me in the foyer –
All except Dario.
At first I felt ashamed, like they were judging me...
And then I saw the sadness in their eyes as Niccolo walked me down the stairs.

Massimo was first.

"Thank you," I whispered. "For saving my life."

"I would do it a thousand times over." He gave me a sad smile. "I had hoped... that you would be around for a long, long time to come."

Tears welled up in my eyes as I smiled back. "So did I."

Next was Roberto.

"We didn't really get a chance to talk much," he said awkwardly, "but you seem like a wonderful person. If there's anything I can help you and your father with in the future... anything with business, anything with money, anything you need... please let me know."

And he pressed a business card into my hand.

"Thank you," I said, and I meant it.

Valentino was next. To my surprise, he reached out and hugged me.

"You're a wonderful girl," he said. "A wonderful woman."

"Will you do me a favor?" I asked.

"What?"

"Try not to break Caterina's heart."

He smiled sadly. "I'll do my best... I promise."

Last up was Adriano. Alone out of all the brothers, he looked angry as I walked up to him – but that was par for the course for him.

I looked at him, unsure what he would say or do –

And then he said simply, "You deserve better than this."

I started crying and smiled. "Thank you."

Out of nowhere, he leaned forward and kissed my forehead like my father might have.

I don't know why, but that affected me the most of all. Tears streamed down my face.

Lars was standing at the end of the line. He looked at me kindly and said, "I'll be the one taking you home. Are you ready?"

I nodded.

He held the front door open.

I looked back at the brothers and smiled through my tears.

*Thank you,* I mouthed silently...

And then I walked out and left them behind forever.

# 46

Dario

I stood in her empty bedroom. The smell of her still lingered in the air.

Niccolo tapped on the door and walked in. "Well... she's gone."

I just nodded in silence.

"Why'd you let her go?" he asked.

"She wanted to leave."

Niccolo gave a bitter laugh. "You weren't so accommodating when she wanted to go to confession a week ago!"

"This is different."

"HOW?! Explain it to me!"

I turned to face him. "What do *you* care? You didn't want me bringing her here in the first place!"

"Well, it's already done, so what does it *matter* what I wanted?"

"Maybe I finally decided to take my *consigliere's* advice," I said mockingly.

"Bullshit. Why can't you just admit what's going on?"

I turned away from him and said nothing.

"It's obvious you're in love with her, you fool," Niccolo snapped. "*I can see it – everyone* else *sees it –* "

"There's no place for love in what we do," I snarled. "Not in the life *we* lead."

"*Bullshit!* You *know* Papa loved Mama – "

"That was a lifetime ago. It's a different world now."

"No, it isn't!" Niccolo shouted. "We inherited it all – the risks are the same, the violence is the same, the life-and-death choices are the same – nothing's different from what our family has faced for generations! So what are you so afraid of?!"

I paused for a second, then said, "Staying here will endanger her."

"Too late! She's already *been* in danger, and she came out the other side unharmed! That's no reason. What the hell is *really* wrong?"

I didn't answer.

"...you think it will make you weak if you love her," Niccolo realized. "You've been don for three weeks, and you're barely hanging on as it is... and you're afraid if you stumble, if you make a mistake, then everything our family fought for will turn to dust... and it'll be *all your fault*. That's it, isn't it? So you're going to play the tragic hero, be miserable and alone, and carry the whole world on your shoulders."

"Fuck you."

"No, FUCK *YOU*. You're my brother – my *family* – and you're forgetting that we're *all in this together*. We stand together, or we fall together – but the important thing is we do it *together*. We do it so the family goes *on* – and how can it go on if you refuse to love? If you refuse to take a wife and have children? Loving Alessandra will make you *stronger*, you idiot. You'll have something greater than yourself to fight for."

"I have the *family* to fight for – "

"There *is no family if it ends with us!*" Niccolo raged. "If we're the last ones... if we die alone... then what the fuck did we sacrifice for?

What the hell is it all worth if there isn't anyone to share it with, to pass it all down to?"

When I didn't answer, Niccolo shook his head. "You're making a terrible mistake. I only hope you realize it in time."

Then he turned and walked out of the room.

I stood there for a long moment...

And then I walked over to the wardrobe where her dresses were still hanging.

I pulled one off the hanger, held it to my face, and breathed deeply.

It smelled of her...

The scent of lilacs...

And the smell of her hair when it was warmed by the sun.

For a second, I imagined she was there with me...

That I hadn't lost her...

And that everything might still be alright.

But then I opened my eyes...

And I was alone and miserable.

Just like Niccolo had said.

# 47

Alessandra

Lars took me back home in one of the Mercedes. It was a 30-minute drive down mostly deserted two-lane roads, and he was quiet most of the way.

I just stared out the window and wondered if I would ever stop hurting.

Finally, he spoke. "It's poetic in a way, isn't it?"

I turned to him, confused. "What is?"

"Our little journey started the moment we saw each other in the café... and now it ends with the two of us, as well."

"I guess that's true," I murmured.

"Is there anything I could say to change your mind? Anything I could do so you'd let me take you back to the house?"

"No. But thank you for asking."

He nodded and continued driving in silence.

Suddenly a thought occurred to me –

And a cold chill went through my body.

Lars was the killer of the group...

The assassin.

He had been the one tasked with shooting the man in the café.

What if he was tasked with doing something *else* tonight?

"...Lars?" I asked, trying to control the fear in my voice.

"Yes?"

"Why were you the one to take me back home?"

"I volunteered."

"Why?"

He shrugged. "Somebody's out there trying to kill Dario and his brothers. They're a target. I'm not."

"I don't think that's true."

He smiled. "Well... it's true they think of me like family... but the fact of the matter is, I'm not as tactically important as any of them. I'm just the muscle. The enforcer, if you will. Plus, I'm better in a firefight than any of them. Dario, Adriano, and Massimo are good, but I'm the best."

"You wouldn't... be taking me out into the country at night... to tie up loose ends, would you?"

He looked over at me in shock –

Then looked back at the road –

And burst out laughing.

"You thought I was driving you somewhere to KILL YOU?!" he said through his laughter.

"Well, I mean, that's what you do, isn't it?"

"No!" he said, sounding offended. "I mean, I kill when I have to, but I do it to protect the family! Plus I would *never* kill women or children – you know that!"

I wanted to say *I know you TOLD me that,* but I didn't think it was wise at the moment.

"What about the man in the café?" I asked.

"Umberto Fumagalli was an enforcer for the Oldanis – a rival family that wants to kill Dario and his brothers so they can take over their territory!"

"So... he basically had the same job as you?"

"Yes – except *I* do it out of necessity. From what I've heard, Fuma-galli enjoyed his work a little too much, if you get my meaning."

My stomach twisted. "...oh."

Lars shook his head ruefully. "I can't believe you thought I was going to *kill* you."

"Well, I mean, you *are* in the mafia."

"Yes, but there's a difference between those who inflict pain and suffering with no regard for innocents, and those who are in a business that happens to be outside the law. That's why Dario insisted they get out of drugs and sex trafficking – because he doesn't want to be part of that anymore. The things he's keeping – gambling and political influence – they're not like taking women out of Eastern Europe and forcing them to be prostitutes. He wants no part of that shit."

"But his father was involved in it," I said.

"And Dario's *stopping* it. In fact, you probably got shot at in Florence because Dario refused to let the Turk do anything in his territory." Lars paused for a second, then shrugged. "Well... *I* think that's what happened, anyway."

"The Turk... Fausto and Dario talked about him a lot."

"I forgot, you were there. Yeah, he was the bastard we had a meeting with while you were in Florence."

We had finally reached a stretch of road that I recognized even in the dark: the street leading up to the village of Mensano.

"My father's place is up here on the right," I said.

"I know," Lars said with a half-smile. "I've been here before, remember?"

"...right..."

He pulled up next to the café. All the lights were out – which made sense, as it was nearly midnight.

Lars pulled out my phone, which I hadn't seen since Dario took it from me the night he'd taken me prisoner.

"Here," he said as he handed it to me. "Do you have a key to get in?"

"I know where the spare is hidden."

"Do you want me to go in with you?"

"No... I'll be fine."

Lars looked into my eyes as though searching for something. "You sure I can't convince you to come back with me? I think you can probably patch things up with Dario."

I smiled sadly and shook my head *no*.

He sighed. "Alright... well, it was worth a shot."

He paused for a second, then continued. "I programmed my personal number into your phone. I know Roberto gave you his card, and he can help you with money – that's his specialty – but *I* can help you if you're ever in danger. If you need anything – anything at all – give me a call, day or night."

"Thank you," I whispered.

He held out a hand as though wanting to shake.

Though a little surprised at how impersonal it seemed, I reached out to take his hand –

But he pulled it back, turned his finger and thumb into a gun, and said *"Pew pew"* like he was shooting the world's quietest pistol.

I gave him a look like *REALLY?!*

Lars laughed out loud. "Sorry – I couldn't resist."

Then he leaned forward and gave me a hug. "Good luck, Alessandra. Call if you need me."

"I will," I promised.

When the hug was over, I got out of the car.

Lars waited until I reached the café and found the spare key hidden in the flower bed.

I unlocked the door and waved.

The Mercedes flashed its lights, pulled out into the road, and drove back the way we had come.

My heart felt heavy as I watched the red taillights disappear into the night...

...and then I went inside and shut the door.

I flicked on the nearest light switch –

And shrieked when I saw a man sitting in the corner, half-hidden in the shadows.

He was unshaven with several days' worth of stubble. A half-empty whiskey bottle sat next to him on the table.

It was my father.

"Papa?!" I cried out, happy and yet bewildered. "What are you doing down here so late?"

He looked up at me with a spark of happiness –

But it was swallowed up by the misery in his eyes.

"My darling," he whispered with a sad smile. "I wish you hadn't come back."

Four men dressed in black stepped out of the shadows.

I shrieked and stumbled backwards –

Just as the door opened behind me and rough hands grabbed my shoulders.

One of the men walked forward into the light.

He was around 45, tall, and dressed in a suit.

He would have been handsome if not for the jagged scar that stretched from his left ear down to the corner of his mouth.

"Alessandra," the man said in a Turkish accent. "So glad you could join us."

# 48

"Sit," the man said.

I had no intention of obeying, but the thug behind me forced me over to Papa's table and into a chair.

I was beginning to think I was the greatest fool ever born for leaving the mansion and Dario's protection.

"Papa, what's going on?!" I asked frantically.

My father looked at me with such despair that it frightened me even more.

"I wish you hadn't come back," he repeated.

"But I, for one, am so glad you did," the man with the scar said. "My name is Mehmet Erdogan – although the Rosolinis probably referred to me as the Turk. Ah, yes – I can see by your face that you know who I am. Good. It was my associate who was gunned down in your café two weeks ago. Seems like such a long time, doesn't it? Tell me, Alessandra – what do the Rosolinis think about what happened that night?"

I looked over at my father –

And the Turk slammed his fist down on the table.

*BAM!*

I flinched and cried out.

"Look at *me,* Alessandra, not him," the Turk instructed. "I'll repeat my question one more time: what do the Rosolinis think about what happened that night?"

"I – I don't know, not for sure, but Lars thinks you're working with some family in Genoa."

"Lars," the Turk said, nodding. "He was the one who gunned down Umberto. Ah, well... Berto should have been faster on the draw. What about the priest and my other associate you encountered last week?"

"I don't *know* what they think," I said quietly, trying to keep my fear under control. "I know Niccolo was trying to find out who they were – but if he did, no one ever told me."

As I spoke, my mind worked at a thousand miles a minute.

How had they known I was coming?!

Or was this all some horrible coincidence?!

"What about the hit in Florence?" the Turk asked. "What are their thoughts on that?"

"They think you did it because Dario wouldn't let you smuggle women through his territory. Or that the family that controls Florence did it for you."

The Turk laughed. "Good. Gooooood."

He sat down between my father and me and poured out a shot of whiskey.

"Would you care for some? No? Ah, that's right... you're a good girl, aren't you?" he said mockingly, then downed the liquor. "Alessandra, tell me... what do *you* think about everything that's happened over the last two weeks?"

"I don't know," I whispered.

"Surely you must have some thoughts. For instance, did poor Umberto say anything to you before he met his untimely end?"

I remembered a detail I hadn't thought of since right after the shooting.

"He said... 'tell your father my compliments to the chef.' Like he knew Papa."

"Because he *did* know your father, Alessandra," the Turk said. "In fact, Umberto and your father were *very* well acquainted."

I stared at Papa.

He wouldn't look back at me. Instead, he just stared at the table.

"How did you know him?" I whispered.

"We'll get there," the Turk said. "But first... don't you find it remarkable that you were in the middle of a gunfight in Florence, yet you never got hit?"

"Massimo saved me."

"Yes... and no. The truth is, *you* saved *Massimo*. You see, my men in Florence – and they *were* my men, although the Agrellas gave their consent – my men were trying *not* to hit *you*. Their highest priority was that you *must* be taken unharmed. Because Massimo kept so close to you, they couldn't concentrate all their firepower on him. They were able to wound him, yes, but they couldn't go all out... not without endangering *you*."

I stared at the Turk in shock.

Was it true?

Had I not been an accidental witness to the violence –

But the reason it had occurred in the first place?

"Why?" I asked in bewilderment.

"Let me tell you a story," the Turk said with a smile. "There once was a young woman who grew up in a family of the *Cosa Nostra*. She was promised to a young man from another family in order to make an alliance. But unbeknownst to her parents, she fell in love with a servant in the household. He was older than her, roughly ten years her senior. Theirs was a forbidden love. If the family had found out, he would have been executed immediately.

"A month before her arranged marriage, the young woman found out she was pregnant. The servant – who loved her more than anything – risked his life to help her escape the city her parents controlled. They fled together with their unborn child and never looked back.

"The family searched for years – in Europe, America, even Russia and the Far East – but no clue ever turned up. Little did they know that their daughter had disappeared by staying *close* to home... right under her family's noses.

"The daughter and her now-husband had a child, a little girl. They raised her near a small village in the middle of nowhere. They were poor, but they were happy. It seemed like things would be fine forever – except the mother died at an early age. Nothing sinister, mind you. No poison, no bullet, no bomb... just an aneurysm. One of those things that could happen to anyone at any time."

I stared at the Turk in shock.

He was describing how my mother had died.

"The former servant continued raising his daughter near the tiny village in Tuscany. He kept her existence secret... and he never let her know that she was actually the granddaughter of one of the most powerful crime families in all of Italy."

"No," I whispered in horror.

I stared at my father, but he would not meet my gaze.

"Yes, my dear," the Turk said with a smile. "You are not Alessandra Calvano. Well, you *are,* since that is the last name your parents chose when they fled Genoa. But you are also Alessandra Oldani, heir to the crime family that has controlled Genoa for generations."

"Why didn't you tell me?" I whispered to my father.

"To keep you safe, my dear," the Turk said. "And to keep *himself* safe. After all, if the family had ever found out where he was, they would have killed him for taking away their daughter... *and* their unborn granddaughter.

"That is where *I* come in.

"As I sought to expand my business dealings outside Turkey, I met with a dozen mafia families throughout Italy. And as I made new allies, I gathered *many* little tidbits of information.

"*I* was the one who heard about a mystery man who sold off rare gold coins every few years in Florence...

"*I* was the one who made the connection between him and the Oldani's mafia princess... who had fled with the servant after stealing a hundred gold coins from her father's safe...

"*I* was the one who sent Umberto Fumagalli here two weeks ago. Umberto had been a young foot soldier in the Oldani household 20 years ago and would know your father by sight.

"What I *didn't* know was the extent of the rivalry between the Oldanis and the Rosolinis. The Rosolinis were one of the few families in Italy I hadn't contacted. I heard the head of their family had died unexpectedly, and his oldest son and heir was still in jail. They were beneath my notice... or so I thought, until they proved themselves both ruthless and efficient. As soon as they found out Umberto was in their territory, they killed him immediately.

"Even worse: they took *you* back to their house, out of my reach. Everything that has transpired since then has been part of my plan to get you back."

"Why?" I asked, horrified. "You plan to give me to the Oldani family – for what? To gain their favor?"

"That was the initial plan, yes," the Turk said. "But another *far* more interesting possibility has arisen."

"And what's that?" I asked angrily.

"When you escaped from the family estate and fled to the church, you did it right under the Rosolinis' noses. How?"

I felt the blood drain from my face.

I couldn't tell him the truth – I *couldn't*.

"They let me," I said. "They knew I was going – "

"That's a lie," the Turk snarled. "While my associate had you pinned down in the alleyway, the priest called my men and repeated everything you'd told him. Don't lie to me again. There is a secret passageway into the Rosolinis' mansion, isn't there?"

"No – "

The Turk slapped me in the face, and I cried out in pain.

My father shouted and tried to stand –

But one of the thugs forced him back down.

"I told you not to lie to me," the Turk said. "The next time you do, I'll leave more than a red mark on your pretty little face. Now – there is a secret passage, yes?"

"Yes... but you'll have to kill me before I'll tell you where it is," I hissed.

The Turk looked at me for a long moment.

"I believe you," he finally said. "I don't think you would betray them, not even to save your own life."

Then he gave me a sinister smile.

"... but I think you might betray them to save someone else's."

The Turk nodded to one of his men, who pulled out a gun and put the barrel against my father's head.

"PAPA!" I screamed.

My father went white as a ghost.

"Now," the Turk said, "you'll take us to the passageway... or I'll have Salvatore here blow out your father's brains."

"Alright – just don't hurt him!" I cried out.

"Good girl," the Turk said with a smile. "I knew you'd see reason."

# 49

And so I led them back to the secret entrance to the mansion.

I had no choice. When they marched me to their parked cars a quarter mile away, they brought Papa, too. They forced him into the front passenger seat while the Turk and I sat in the back.

The entire drive, the Turk held a gun to the back of my father's head.

"If you cross me, you get to watch him die," the Turk warned.

"I can lead you to the secret door, but it locks from the inside," I said frantically. "There's no way to get back in."

"You just get me there. I'll do the rest."

I had hoped that maybe I could text Lars a warning – but the first thing they did was confiscate my cell phone.

"Don't want you stabbing us in the back," the Turk smirked.

*Stabbing us in the back.*

That's what I would be doing to Dario, Massimo, and all the others:

I would be leading their greatest enemy right to them in the dead of night.

I *hated* myself for doing it. I would have given almost anything to *not* do it, including my own life –

But I would not sacrifice my father.

I couldn't.

I just prayed that God would somehow find a way to let Dario and the others know what was happening.

The one kindness the Turk allowed me was he let me hold my father's hand through the gap in the front seats.

"I'm so sorry, Alessandra," my father whispered.

"It's alright, Papa," I said through my tears.

"I always wanted to tell you... but I wanted you to be safe..."

"It's okay, Papa. It's all going to be okay."

"And it will," the Turk agreed, interrupting the heartfelt moment. Then he gave me an evil smile. "As long as you give me everything I want."

I didn't believe him.

I wasn't sure what would happen. Maybe he would give me to the Oldanis, so I could become the prisoner of *another* mafia family –

But I didn't see the Turk letting my father go free.

What could I do, though, with him holding a gun to Papa's head?

The Turk's men drove into the village and parked at the base of the hill, the one leading up to the ten-foot stone wall with the crack in it.

When we got out of our car, the Turk pointed at Papa. "Tie him up and throw him in the trunk."

Two thugs grabbed my father and started binding his hands and legs.

"No!" I cried out.

"What did you *think* would happen?" the Turk asked me. "That I'd leave him here to cause mischief? He can either go in the trunk, or we can shoot him. Which do you prefer?"

"Don't hurt him," I whispered.

"It's alright," my father reassured me. "Everything will be alright."

"Spoken like a true optimist," the Turk said.

Then his men threw Papa in the trunk and shut it tight.

"Now," the Turk said, gesturing with his gun. "Lead the way."

Fourteen of us went up the hillside – me, the Turk, and 12 of his men.

Every man but the Turk had a pistol with a silencer attached to it.

The Turk's gun was short and stubby – the better to press up against his victim's head.

Except that he let *me* walk ahead of them like a dog.

The gun pointed at my back was my leash.

I did my best to retrace my path in the darkness. Once I got to the wall, I had to search for several minutes before I finally found the crack.

"Here it is," I said. "But aren't you afraid of cameras?"

"There *are* no cameras back here," the Turk said confidently. "There haven't been for the last 50 years."

I stared at him. "How do you know that?"

He smiled. "I have my sources."

One of the Turk's men went through the gap first. He pointed his gun at me as I went next so I wouldn't run away.

One by one, the others followed until all 14 of us were through.

I thought about what would happen once we got close to the house.

If I screamed, would Dario or anyone else even hear me?

I would be killed instantly – I knew that – but at least they would know someone was coming.

However, the Turk would probably retreat...

...and then shoot my father in the head as punishment for my betrayal.

Still, I weighed my options about screaming...

Until the Turk took even *that* choice away from me.

He ripped a piece of duct tape off a roll and said, "Close your lips."

I did as I was told, and he taped over my mouth.

"Good. Now take us there," the Turk commanded.

I backtracked through the woods until I reached the end of the trees.

The Rosolini mansion stood dark and still in the moonlight, almost 600 feet away...

...and I was helpless to warn them.

I walked as far as I thought was correct, then got down on all fours. I crawled along, fumbling with my hands in the ferns and undergrowth –

Until my hand slipped all the way through a patch of vines.

I thought for a second about not telling the Turk and hoping his men missed it completely...

...but if he found out I lied to him, he would kill my father out of spite.

So I turned and gestured at the ground.

The Turk nodded, and two of his thugs tore up the vines to reveal a hole in the ground. Others shone flashlights at the stone steps, and we entered the underground passageway.

When we reached the iron door, one of the men tried the handle. It refused to budge.

I looked at the Turk and gestured like *See? I told you!*

He just grinned.

"If I let something as simple as *this* stop me, I never would have gotten anywhere in life." Then he barked, "Do it!"

Two of the men duct-taped bags of dark powder to the hinges on the door.

"Thermite powder," the Turk said with a chuckle. "The Allies used it in World War II to destroy the largest artillery gun the Nazis ever created. It can cut through four inches of steel like it was nothing."

A third man lit a small blowtorch and set one of the bags on fire.

"Stand back," the Turk said as he pulled me far away.

Suddenly the bag began to burn as bright as the sun, throwing off sparks everywhere.

I cried out, but the duct tape over my mouth muffled the sound.

The Turk cackled in delight.

Once the sparks died away, a glowing hole was all that was left where the hinge had once been.

"Light the other one," the Turk ordered.

They repeated the process. Once it was over and the hinges were destroyed, the thugs used a crowbar to pry off the door. Five strong men caught the massive slab of metal and lowered it to the ground.

"Let us continue," the Turk said, and we walked through the doorway into the darkness.

# 50

As we continued down the stone tunnel, it felt like I was in a horror movie.

The thugs' flashlight beams barely lit our way...

The Turk's gun pressed into the back of my head...

And every step brought me closer to betraying the man I loved.

His death – and his brothers' deaths – would be all my fault.

We finally reached the servants' passageway.

From there, it was just 20 paces to the secret door near the chapel.

Once we were in the hallway, the thugs formed a protective circle with me and the Turk at the center. Their footsteps tapped lightly on the tiled floors as they moved through the dark house.

Then we reached the grand staircase in the foyer.

"Go," the Turk whispered.

Six men went up the stairs, pistols at the ready.

I realized that there was one gunman for each brother –

Adriano, Massimo, Roberto, Niccolo, Valentino...

...and Dario.

As I stood there with tears streaming down my face, I wanted to scream and warn them – but it wouldn't have done any good.

The tape over my mouth would have muffled any sound I made –

and there were still six thugs around me and the Turk. Any one of them would kill me if I made the slightest sound.

I just prayed that one of the brothers would hear the assassins and alert the others...

...before it was too late.

"In just a moment," the Turk whispered in my ear, "all six Rosolinis will be dead, and their empire will be – "

He never finished the sentence because gunshots cut him off.

I could see the muzzle flashes in the dark all around us.

*BANG BANG BANG BANG BANG!*

I shrieked under the tape on my mouth, sure that I would die –

But it was the Turk's men who dropped to the ground dead.

"WHAT?!" the Turk roared.

He pulled me up against him as a human shield and pressed his gun to my right temple.

Three men dressed in black came out of the darkness, their pistols pointed right at us.

Adriano...

Valentino...

And Dario.

"Let her go," Dario said quietly, his voice steady.

"STOP!" the Turk screamed. "STOP, OR I'LL KILL HER!"

Dario put his arms up and pointed his pistol at the ceiling. "Adriano, Valentino... lower your guns and get back."

Adriano tried to protest. "But – "

"DO IT."

Adriano and Valentino pointed their guns at the floor, then slowly stepped backwards into the shadows.

"There," Dario said. "They've backed off. Now let her go."

The Turk laughed. "I don't think so."

"If you let her go, I'll let you walk out of here unharmed. You have my word."

"Your *word*," the Turk sneered. "Do you think I'm stupid?"

"No, but you must think *I* am. Otherwise, why would you keep stalling?"

The Turk didn't say anything.

"Do you hear that?" Dark asked.

There was only silence.

"There's nothing to hear," the Turk snapped.

"Exactly. All the men you sent upstairs are dead," Dario said. "My brothers killed your assassins upstairs at the exact same moment we shot your men down here. It's over. Let her go."

The Turk became enraged. He tightened his left arm around my neck and jammed his gun harder into my skull.

"You fucking bitch traitor!" he hissed in my ear.

"She had nothing to do with it," Dario said. "We were watching you on camera from the moment you came through the wall."

The Turk wheezed like he had been punched. "But... there weren't supposed to *be* any cameras..."

"Did you really think I would leave my entire estate unguarded? Now, stop pointing your gun at her... and aim it at me."

The Turk stepped backwards and dragged me along with him.

"Aim your gun at me," Dario repeated calmly.

I could hardly see him anymore, my eyes were so blurry with tears.

"Why bother?" the Turk hissed. "You'll kill me no matter what."

"No, I won't – and neither will my brothers. I swear on my father's grave."

"And why should I believe you?"

"Because I'll take her place," Dario said calmly.

I tried to scream *NO!* beneath the tape over my mouth.

"Shhh, it's fine," he said to me in a calm voice, then looked back at the Turk. "Take me hostage, and you'll walk out of here a free man. All you have to do is aim your gun at me, not her."

The Turk hesitated – then demanded, "Get rid of your pistol first."

"Alright... don't shoot."

Dario leaned over slowly, set his gun on the floor, and kicked it gently over to the Turk. Then he held up his hands.

"I'm defenseless. Take your gun away from her... and aim it at me."

I could hear the Turk breathing behind my ear.

I could feel the barrel of his gun pressed against my head.

Suddenly the pressure went away, and I saw the gun swing out over my shoulder towards Dario.

I screamed into the duct tape covering my mouth.

"Fool," the Turk snarled –

And then there was a single flash of light up on the second floor, a muffled *PTOK* –

And the Turk fell away from me, his arm sliding off my neck.

I stood there trembling as the bastard's body thudded on the floor behind me.

# 51

Dario raced towards me and wrapped me up in his strong arms.

I hung onto him, finally safe.

After a second, he pulled away so he could see my face.

"Are you alright?" he whispered.

I nodded.

He smiled at me, happier than I had ever seen him before. "Let's not ever do that again."

I laughed behind the tape on my mouth.

"Is everyone all right?" Dario yelled as he felt for the edge of the tape on my face.

"We're fine!" someone yelled from the third floor – Massimo, by the sound of it.

"This is going to hurt," Dario warned me right before he peeled the tape off my face.

But after everything I had been through, the pain was nothing.

As soon as the tape was off, he asked, "Are you really okay?"

"Yes!" I cried out happily, tears streaming down my cheeks –

And he kissed me passionately.

I wrapped my arms around his neck and kissed him back as hard as I could.

"Hey – get a room!" Niccolo's voice called down from the second floor.

Dario and I broke off the kiss and laughed.

I looked up to see Niccolo, Massimo, and Roberto on the second floor, dressed in black and beaming. Behind them were another dozen armed men, the foot soldiers of the Rosolini family. They were cheering and giving each other high-fives.

Another figure came down the stairs, a high-powered rifle slung over his shoulder. He pulled off his black balaclava to reveal a shock of blond hair.

"Are you alright?" Lars asked me worriedly.

"What, you couldn't see that from the kiss?" Niccolo shouted from above.

"I'm fine!" I assured Lars.

He looked strained and haggard. "That was the most stressful shot of my entire life."

Dario put his hand on Lars's shoulder. "I knew you could do it. That's why I entrusted it to you."

Lars nodded, and I hugged him. He finally relaxed and laughed as he hugged me back.

"Can we bring everyone out?" Valentino asked.

"You just want to look like the big hero," Niccolo teased him.

"Hey, you heard her earlier," Valentino said as he pointed at me. "She *told* me to take care of my lady!"

"Fine, whatever," Niccolo said.

Valentino went down the hall and opened up a door. "It's alright – you're safe – you can come out now!"

Two dozen servants streamed into the hall, including a handful of armed foot soldiers who had been guarding them.

The servants were all dressed in pajamas like they had been pulled out of their beds just moments before.

Caterina was among them. She ran into Valentino's arms, and he kissed her as he swung her around in the air.

Lars went over to control the crowd.

"What happened?" I asked Dario as I stared at the servants.

"When we saw you were coming on the surveillance cameras, we got everyone out of bed," he explained. "But we couldn't risk taking anyone outside in case the Turk noticed... so we hid them and had my men protect them."

In an instant, I remembered my role in all of this. "I'm sorry, Dario – I'm so sorry – they had my father – "

"Shh, shh, it's okay," he whispered. "None of this would have happened if I'd hadn't been a fool and let you go."

I broke down sobbing in his arms as he held me.

"It's alright," he murmured in my ear. "I'm never letting you go ever again."

Then I thought of something else. "My father – he's in the trunk of one of the cars at the base of the hill!"

"We'll send someone right away," Dario promised, then turned around. "Adriano, her father's in one of the Turk's cars – take some men down there and free him."

"Should I search the bodies up here for keys?" Adriano asked.

Dario moved away from me as he and Adriano discussed searching the Turk's men for keys.

That's when I saw her.

Filomena.

The old woman moved like a sleepwalker out of the crowd of servants, her frail body draped in a white nightgown down to her ankles.

I thought she might look at me, and I dreaded meeting her gaze –

But something was wrong.

Her eyes were fixed on Dario and nothing else.

My eyes dropped to her arm by her side.

It was hard to see because of the servants and people criss-crossing between us –

But I finally spied something small and black in her hand.

A gun.

She was 12 feet away from Dario and getting closer.

If I shouted, there was no guarantee that they would know who to shoot –

And if I screamed her name, it would alert her –

And she might take the shot.

I had only a second to act –

And I made my choice.

I bent down and grabbed the gun that Dario had kicked over to the Turk.

I prayed that it was no more complicated than I had seen in the movies –

And I began to walk towards her as fast as I could.

Filomena started to raise her arm.

No one saw except me –

Because no one suspected an old woman would kill anyone.

Niccolo saw, though it was too late.

"GUN!" he screamed as he reached for his holstered pistol –

But by that time Filomena was only six feet away from Dario. Her arm raised the gun towards his head –

Which is when I fired.

*BANG!*

She jerked and fell to the floor.

Dario glanced down at her in shock, then looked at me with wide eyes.

I stood staring down at her body, the gun shaking in my hands as smoke curled up into the air.

## 52

Chaos erupted.

Servants ran screaming from the room.

Lars ran over and kicked away the tiny pistol that had fallen from Filomena's hand.

As I continued to stare down at her, Dario took my gun away from me gently.

Then he whispered in my ear, "Thank you, *amore mio*. You saved my life."

I burst out crying, and he hugged me to his body.

The entire time, Filomena stared up at us hatefully.

She was still alive. Her chest moved slowly up and down, even as a puddle of red spread on the floor beneath her.

Valentino pushed Caterina towards the safety of another room, then turned back to the rest of us.

"What the fuck just happened?!" Adriano yelled as he ran over.

"I think that's our mole," Niccolo shouted as he, Massimo, and Roberto ran down the stairs.

"...a mole?" I asked in shock.

"She told you how to get out of the house, didn't she?" Niccolo asked.

I nodded and sobbed. "I'm so sorry... I should have told you..."

"Eh... 20/20 hindsight," he said grimly. "I *should* be angry with you, but it exposed a gaping hole in our defenses. We thought only the family knew about the passageway. Stupid of us. So we installed cameras to ensure no one could ever take us by surprise again... and that's how we saw you and the Turk."

"He was waiting for me at my father's place," I said.

"She probably called him as soon as you left," Dario said as he gazed down at Filomena.

Suddenly I was hit with an epiphany. *Everything* became clear in a flash.

"*She* was the one who made me want to leave!" I cried out. "She told me I was a whore, and how my mother and father would have been ashamed of me! She planned this – ALL of this!"

I hated her at that instant –

But not as much Dario hated her.

I had never seen such fury on his face as he stared down at Filomena.

"I swear to God," he seethed, "if you weren't an old woman, I'd blow your brains out on the floor."

"Don't let that stop you, you *pezzo di merda,*" she hissed, blood bubbling out of her mouth.

"Oh-ho, Granny's got a mouth on her!" Niccolo said as he squatted down beside her. "You were in league with the Turk the entire time, weren't you?"

Filomena glared up at him with a hatred as hot as the sun. "Of course I was."

"Why didn't you just *tell* him how to get in? Why involve Alessandra?"

"Someone had to show them the way," she sneered.

It was true. I'd only found the secret entrance in the dark because I was retracing my steps.

"Why did you do it?" Dario asked angrily. "For money?"

"No."

"Then *why?*"

"Because your father had my husband and son killed," she snarled... and then she began to laugh. "Which is why I killed *him*."

Silence fell over the room except for the old woman's ragged breathing.

"...what?" Niccolo whispered.

"You're lying," Dario said, his voice shaking.

Filomena grinned, her teeth stained crimson. "I injected him with sodium nitrate... and you fools thought he had a heart attack. Well... I guess he did. Just not a natural one."

"You fucking – " Adriano roared as he pulled his gun to shoot her –

But Dario grabbed his hand and stopped him.

"Why did my father have your husband and son killed?" he asked the old woman.

"Why do *any* of your kind do anything? For money. For power. For years I mourned their deaths... and then I decided to do something about it. I wormed my way into your father's service... and became a trusted servant. When I killed him, I whispered into his ear... 'For my family, you son of a whore.'"

"You didn't get a job here without help," Dario said. "And the Turk couldn't have done something like that – so who did?"

Filomena just laughed and spat blood on his feet.

Dario squatted down next to her. "You *will* tell me who helped you... or I promise you will live to regret it."

"My only regret," she snarled, "is that I didn't get to kill *you*, too."

Then she bit down on something in her mouth.

Blood-tinted froth began to spill from her lips –

Just like the priest and the thug who had attacked me outside the church.

"Stop her!" Dario yelled.

He put his finger in her mouth and tried to fish out the cyanide capsule –

But it was too late.

Her body jerked a couple of times... and then she was gone.

# 53

After Filomena's shocking death, the foot soldiers removed all the bodies from the house, and the servants began to clean up the blood.

While they did that, Adriano went with a half-dozen men to set my father free.

I wasn't there to see it – I stayed at the house at Dario's insistence – but Papa said later he almost died of fright when the trunk opened up.

Adriano calmed him down and told him everything was alright – and that I was alive and unhurt.

When he got to the house, Papa hugged me and started sobbing. "I'm so sorry, Alessandra… I should have told you…"

"It's alright," I comforted him, then introduced him to the six brothers and Lars. "They saved my life – multiple times."

My father thanked them all profusely. Everyone was kind to him, which I appreciated more than I could say –

Especially since Papa and I were the reason their house had been invaded by murderers in the middle of the night.

After my father thanked them, Niccolo asked, "What were you saying earlier? About what you should have told her?"

"Oh," I said. "About that..."

I repeated everything the Turk had told me: how my father and mother had escaped 20 years earlier...

And how the Turk had planned to use me as a pawn to get the Oldanis as his allies.

My father confirmed the parts that involved him, including his and my mother's escape from Genoa.

Everyone was astonished –

Although Dario seemed the least shocked.

"So you're a mafia princess?" he asked in amusement.

"I wouldn't call myself *that,*" I said distastefully.

"I think your grandparents might."

Grandparents...

I had never met them. Papa had told me both his parents and my mother's parents had died before I was born.

The idea that some of them were still alive, but were in the *Cosa Nostra...*

I didn't know how I felt about that.

"Wait... so the Genoans were never out to get us?" Valentino asked in astonishment.

"Let's not jump to conclusions," Niccolo cautioned. "We have no idea how much the Turk said was true. His discovery about Alessandra's heritage might have conveniently overlapped with the Oldanis' desire to wipe us out."

"Please, sir," my father begged Dario, "you have to protect me – the Oldanis will *kill* me for what I did!"

Dario put his arm around me. "Your daughter is under my protection, and thus *you* are under my protection. No harm will come to you, I promise."

I snuggled up under Dario's arm. To me, it was the safest place in the world.

My father didn't seem *quite* as happy to see us so close.

Probably because of what Dario had said in the café.

You know...

The part about not taking my virginity until I begged him to do it.

But then Dario surprised us both.

"I have something to ask you," he said to my father, who turned white as a sheet.

He probably thought Dario would demand some sort of mafia favor, like burying bodies on his property.

To be truthful, I thought the exact same thing.

Then Dario told my father, "I would like your blessing to marry Alessandra."

Just about everyone in the room gasped (me included) –

Except for Dario and Niccolo.

Niccolo grinned and handed a tiny object to Dario that I couldn't see.

"I... I..." my father stuttered, then turned to me. "If she wishes to marry you, then yes, I give my blessing!"

I turned to Dario in disbelief –

At which point, he knelt down in front of me and took my hand.

"Alessandra... when you left earlier... that was the first time I realized I loved you. Madly... passionately... deeply. You are the only thing that has brought me true happiness. And when I nearly lost you tonight... I realized that I couldn't live without you. I love you, and I never want to part from you ever again. Will you marry me?"

I burst out crying – with happy tears, this time! – and nodded *yes* as I smiled and laughed.

The brothers all cheered.

Adriano, Massimo, Roberto, Niccolo, Valentino –

And Lars. By now, I thought of him as one of the brothers, too.

Dario grinned and held out a stunning diamond ring. It looked old-fashioned, with tiny rubies and pearls in a setting around the diamond.

I gasped at the sight of it and realized it was the object Niccolo had given him just moments before.

"It was my mother's," Dario told me, then glanced at his brothers. "I hope you don't mind."

They all cheered again and yelled their approval.

"You know you have *my* blessing," Niccolo said.

Adriano grinned, the first time I had ever seen a smile on his face. "I can't think of anyone I would rather see wear Mama's ring."

I cried even harder at his words –

And then Dario slipped the ring on my finger, stood up, and kissed me.

For a moment, the world stopped... and I felt like I was in a fairy tale.

Then I was brought back to reality as everyone clapped: the brothers, the family's foot soldiers, and the servants who had heard the commotion and come to see what was going on.

Dario smiled at me, and I beamed up at him.

All the brothers gathered round to congratulate us. They hugged me and slapped Dario on the shoulder.

Niccolo was the last.

"So good to have you as my sister," he said as he hugged me. "I always wanted one... and now I do."

I hugged him back. "I always wanted a brother... and now I have six!"

Valentino laughed. "Did you hear that, Lars? You're an honorary sibling!"

"I better be after tonight," Lars joked.

Niccolo sighed theatrically. "A true *Cosa Nostra* engagement – love and death in equal measure. All the men beside Alessandra's father, follow me – we have some graves to dig in the orchards!"

Then my brother-in-law-to-be looked at me and winked. "Don't worry – I promise the wedding will be a *bit* more conventional."

## 54

While Dario, Niccolo, and the other men toiled in the moonlight, I sat in the parlor with my father. There were so many questions I had.

Once he had answered them all, Papa asked, "I have to know... are you sure this is the life you want?"

I knew what he meant:

The *Cosa Nostra.*

My father had fled from the mafia to be with the woman he loved...

And now I was marrying into it to be with the man *I* loved.

"I don't know about the life itself... but I want Dario," I said. "And I would do anything to be with him."

Papa smiled. "I felt the same about your mother. I knew it would mean a life of hiding and secrecy... but I couldn't live without her."

Dario sent word to the house that it would be hours before they were finished and that my father and I should go to bed.

A servant arrived to take Papa to his own room at the opposite end of the house.

"Why so far from mine?" I whispered to the woman.

She smiled and whispered back, "So he won't hear you when you're with Don Rosolini."

I blushed bright red –

But I had to admit, it was good foresight on her part.

After hugging Papa goodnight, I went back to my room and showered. Then I slipped into bed and fell asleep, exhausted.

I awoke at dawn as Dario slipped under the sheets beside me.

He had showered, too, and his hair was still damp. The only thing he was wearing was a pair of black boxers.

"Is everything alright?" I murmured sleepily.

"Yes. Everything's taken care of." He smiled at the ring on my finger as it twinkled in the early morning sun. "I like seeing you wear that."

"Good... because it's the *only* thing I'm wearing," I said mischievously.

He raised one of his eyebrows. "Really."

His hands roved under the sheets, and I felt his fingers brush against my breasts.

Immediately my nipples became hard at his touch.

He moved to kiss me –

But I stopped him by placing a finger on his lips.

"I have one thing to ask you," I whispered.

He peered deep into my eyes. "What?"

"Our children..."

He grinned. "I like the sound of that."

I smiled back. "I do, too."

Then I grew serious.

"But I don't want their father handing a pistol to my son when he's 15 years old. I don't want that for *any* of them. When Fausto was here, Roberto said the family would be legitimate in two years. Can you promise me that our children won't have to be in danger like you and your brothers were? That they'll be safe?"

Dario nodded somberly. "I swear upon my family's name that they will not follow in my footsteps. They will inherit an entirely new life... one where they can be doctors, or lawyers, or actors, or artists, or anything else they want to be... but not *mafiosos.*"

I smiled and teared up a little. "Thank you."

He kissed me softly...

And I reached down to his boxers and began to pull them off.

"I like this new side of you," he said with a grin.

"I want *lots* of babies, so you're going to have to make love to me *a lot.*"

He laughed. "Absolutely. Starting *right now.*"

## 55

The wedding was only two weeks later. Dario said he didn't want a long engagement – just enough to arrange everything. I happily agreed.

Security was 'all hands on deck' as every Rosolini foot soldier patrolled the property. Massimo and Valentino strolled the grounds dressed in tuxes and carrying guns. Even Roberto, who was usually much more like an accountant, kept a pistol inside his suit jacket.

Lars kept watch from the top of the mansion with his sniper rifle. He had saved me from the Turk that awful night as Dario posed as bait and put his own life in danger; I liked the idea of Lars watching over us again under much happier circumstances.

Fausto and Aurelio arrived with an even larger convoy of cars, and dozens of their foot soldiers helped Dario's men guard the property.

Niccolo had brokered a truce with the Oldani family in Genoa. I met my long-lost relatives with Niccolo at my side since Dario couldn't see me before I came down the aisle.

As I walked down the stairs into the foyer, I choked up when I saw an older woman with white hair in a beautiful blue dress. She looked so much like my mother that it was astounding.

The woman's mouth dropped open when she saw me. "*È un miracolo!*"

*It's a miracle!*

"Signora Oldani," Niccolo said with a smile, "may I present your granddaughter... Alessandra."

The old woman touched one hand tenderly to my cheek and began to cry. "You look so much like your mother – I can't believe it!"

I hugged her tight. "Thank you for coming... it means so much to me..."

"Of course – I wouldn't have missed it for the world!" Then her voice grew stern. "Although I'm going to have a few words with that father of yours – "

"Signora," Niccolo said lightly, "remember: it's her wedding day. Play nice."

The older woman gave Niccolo a dirty look – but when she *did* meet Papa afterwards, she was civil.

Out on the grounds of the estate milled dozens of distinguished-looking men and their beautiful wives... but I had never seen any of them before.

"Who *are* all these people?" I whispered to Niccolo.

"*Cosa Nostra,*" he whispered back. "The heads of the most powerful families in Italy."

I frowned. "I thought you had a lot of enemies."

"Oh, don't be mistaken – most of these people want us dead," Niccolo said as he waved and fake-smiled at someone far away. "But we *had* to invite them. You have to keep up appearances in this line of work – and you know what they say about keeping your friends close and your enemies closer."

When Niccolo saw my face, he chuckled. "Don't worry, they would *never* do anything on your wedding day. It would be an *infamia.*"

*An infamy* – a wicked, horrible thing.

"Plus, we didn't let their guards bring in any guns... so we'd just kill them," Niccolo said cheerfully as he waved at someone else.

"Wonderful," I muttered.

Caterina was my only female friend, so I'd asked her to be my maid of honor two weeks before. She had immediately said yes.

Now she beamed at me as the makeup artist from Rome put the final touches on me before the ceremony.

"You look so beautiful," Cat sighed. "Like a fairytale princess."

"Maybe you'll get your *own* fairytale prince!"

"Not gonna lie – you've given me hope," she grinned. "If *you* can snag a Rosolini…"

Finally it was time for the ceremony, which took place in the field behind the mansion. Gorgeous flower arrangements lined the white chairs set out for the attendees.

But I didn't look at any of them as my beaming father walked me down the aisle.

I only had eyes for Dario.

He stood at the altar in a tuxedo and a small white rose pinned to his lapel.

He smiled at me as I came down the aisle. I had never seen him look happier – or more handsome.

Adriano was his best man. The other brothers would have served as groomsmen, but I only had one bridesmaid. Everyone else agreed they wanted to make sure the wedding was safe as possible.

"That'll be our present to you," Massimo had joked the night before the wedding.

To me, it wasn't a joke. Their protectiveness was a sign of their love for me.

The priest – a cardinal from the Vatican – led the ceremony.

When he said, "You may now kiss the bride," Dario wrapped his arms around me and gave me a kiss that made everyone in the audience cheer.

## 56

A s beautiful as the wedding was, the dinner afterwards was even better. The tables were outside, and we enjoyed the fading twilight as the gorgeous hills of Tuscany lit up with violet and amber skies.

People drank and laughed and feasted. Children played and chased each other in the gardens.

I talked some more with my grandmother, who told me stories about my mother when she was a child.

My father got drunk and bonded with Massimo and Niccolo. They all laughed uproariously.

The only slightly sour note was when Fausto came up to congratulate us. Thankfully Aurelio stayed away.

"You look beautiful," Fausto told me as he air-kissed my cheeks.

"Thank you," I said as pleasantly as I could.

I remembered his last visit to the estate too well to be *too* friendly with him.

"And you – congratulations to you, nephew," he said to Dario.

"I think you mean *'Don Rosolini,'*" Niccolo said pointedly.

"He's Don Rosolini, *I'm* Don Rosolini – it all cancels out," Fausto said good-naturedly.

"Not when you hand out advice as bad as *you* do," Niccolo snarked.

Fausto sighed in resignation. "The part about me saying the Turk wasn't behind it?"

"That would be it."

"You're never going to let me live that down, are you?"

"No, I'm *not.*"

"We're all allowed to be wrong once in a while."

"Not when my wife's life is on the line," Dario said coldly.

I liked when Dario said *my wife.*

"Well, she seems well enough now," Fausto said smugly. "Ordinarily, I would say she's come up in the world – from a waitress in a café to a wife in the *Cosa Nostra.* But seeing as she's a granddaughter of the Oldanis, it might be *you* that's come up in the world, my boy. Forging an alliance like *that* – "

"Fausto?" Dario interrupted.

"Yes?"

"Good to see you," Dario said. He patted his uncle on the shoulder and then turned away, dismissing him abruptly.

Fausto chuckled. "Be careful, Dario. You might need my help someday."

"Not today, though," Niccolo said. "Say hello to Aurelio for us. Or you know what? ...don't."

Fausto glared at Niccolo and Dario but walked off without saying another word.

"Was that wise?" I asked Dario.

"Look who has a new *consigliere!*" Niccolo said with a laugh. "Maybe you'll listen to *her* more than you ever listened to *me!*"

I gave my husband a reproving look. "Is it smart to be so rude to your uncle?"

"A better question, my love," Dario said as he kissed my cheek, "is whether he was smart to be so rude towards *us.*"

"We're no longer his teenage nephews," Niccolo said. "The sooner he comes to terms with that, the better."

## 57

L ater in the evening, all the brothers came over to me and Dario.

"Are you ready for the honeymoon?" Lars asked.

"Can't wait," Dario said.

"Are you and Massimo still coming along?" I asked.

"Of course," Lars said.

Massimo smiled. "Somebody has to protect the don and his blushing bride on their honeymoon so they can relax."

"Don't worry, they'll stay far enough away that they can't hear you at night," Valentino teased.

I smacked him with my bouquet of flowers.

"Is that even possible?" Roberto asked. "They would have to be *miles* away!"

I hit Roberto even harder, and both he and Valentino laughed.

I looked over and saw Dario and Adriano talking quietly amongst themselves.

I didn't catch everything, but I *did* hear something about 'Florence' and 'the Agrellas.'

When Dario and Adriano came back over, I asked, "Is everything alright?"

"Yes."

"What were you two talking about?"

Dario replied, "When we return from the honeymoon, Massimo and Lars will go with Adriano to Florence."

"Why?"

"To talk to the Agrellas."

"Who send their kindest regards but sadly couldn't be here tonight," Niccolo said with false saccharine sweetness and a mocking smile.

"Adriano's going to reestablish our territory," Dario explained. "He'll serve as our family's *capo* in Florence."

*Capo* meant 'boss' and was short for *caporegime.*

Like *consigliere,* it was another term for the hierarchy within the mafia.

It meant that Adriano would become the family's representative in Florence...

...*if* he didn't start a war first.

"It's fine," Adriano said reassuringly. "The Agrellas are nothing. Plus I'll have Lars and Massimo with me."

I still felt worried.

These were my new brothers-in-law, after all.

"No more business talk tonight!" Niccolo said. "A toast – to the bride and groom!"

"To the bride and groom!" all of the brothers cheered.

We talked and laughed and went around to each of the tables so Dario could greet both friends and enemies –

When we saw Valentino slip off with a giggling Caterina into the nearby gardens.

"Now *they* have the right idea," Dario murmured in my ear.

"Don't you need to say hello to more people?"

"I think I'd rather start the honeymoon early."

He led me back to the house, where we slipped upstairs to his bedroom.

I started to take off my clothes –

"No," he said in a lustful voice, "I want to fuck you in your wedding dress."

I laughed. "Standing up?!"

"Standing up," he growled.

I gasped as he reached under my dress and pulled my panties down to my ankles. That still left my stockings and garter belt.

I quickly unzipped his pants and pulled out his cock, which was only halfway hard...

But I felt his manhood grow thicker and longer in my hand by the second.

The feeling was indescribably sexy...

And I luxuriated in stroking him to full hardness as we kissed.

I couldn't stand the anticipation for much longer.

"I need you inside me," I whispered.

"And I *need* to be inside you," he murmured in my ear.

He gathered up the bunches of my wedding dress...

And lifted me effortlessly into the air with one hand under my bare ass and the other around my waist.

I moaned as I wrapped my legs around his waist.

He pressed me up against the wall...

And kissed me as he slowly eased the swollen head of his cock into my pussy.

I moaned as he entered an inch, then pulled back.

With his shaft now wet with my juices, he slid in a little bit more and withdrew.

Inch by inch, he sank deeper and deeper inside me...

Until he filled me up completely.

We had never done it standing up, with him lifting me in the air so easily –

And certainly not in a wedding dress and tux.

We French-kissed as he rocked in and out of me.

Pleasure slowly built inside of me with every stroke.

He had a way of grinding his pelvis against me that rubbed deliciously against my clit...

All while his cock moved deep inside me.

And he was *sooo* thick...

I was moaning, getting closer and closer to an orgasm, when he pulled back enough to look at me.

"How close are you?" he asked as rocked back and forth inside me.

My eyes wanted to roll back in my head, but I forced myself to look at him.

"So close," I moaned.

"Don't come yet."

"Ohhhh – " I complained.

*"Don't come yet."*

His deep voice was so commanding that I *had* to obey.

"Alright," I gasped as I struggled not to tip over the edge.

"Will you do something for me, *amore mio?* For our wedding day?"

"Anything," I moaned. "Anything..."

I was so close –

Right on the edge –

It was so hard to hold back –

Then he leaned over and whispered in my ear, "Will you come for me... *Signora* Rosolini?"

With those words, he made me come harder – and scream louder – than I ever had before.


MAFIA KINGS: ADRIANO
is now available on Amazon!


If you enjoyed DARIO, would you please leave a review or rating? It would help me more than you know! Thank you!


Free Epilogue -
Read about Dario and Alessandra's honeymoon!

I hope you enjoyed MAFIA KINGS: DARIO. I have a very special and exclusive free offer for you! Every book in the series will have an epilogue you can only get if you join my mailing list.

You'll be the first to know when each new book in the series is available – plus every book, you'll get a new epilogue that you *can't* get anywhere else. The first one for DARIO is about Alessandra and Dario's honeymoon.

To read it,
go to www.oliviathorn.com!

# ABOUT THE AUTHOR

Check out my website to get on my mailing list and receive the Epilogue to MAFIA KINGS: DARIO!

www.oliviathorn.com

You can find me on Facebook at...

https://www.facebook.com/oliviathornbooks

And feel free to drop me a line at

olivia@oliviathorn.com

# ALSO BY OLIVIA THORN

Mafia Kings: Dario

Mafia Kings: Adriano

Mafia Kings: Massimo

Mafia Kings: Lars (coming soon)

\*\*\*

**AS OLIVIA THORNE**

**Billionaire Romance**

All That He Wants (Volume 1)

All That He Loves (Volume 2)

The Billionaire's Wedding (Volume 3)

\*\*\*

The Billionaire's Kiss (Parts 1-4)

The Billionaire's Obsession (Part 5)

\*\*\*

**Motorcycle Romance**

Midnight Desire (Part 1)

Midnight Lust (Part 2)

Midnight Deceit (Part 3)

Midnight Obsession (Part 4)

\*\*\*

**Rockstar Romance**

(Careful - cheating in Part 3, Why Choose, HFN ending)

Rock Me Hard (Part 1)

Rock All Night (Part 2)

Hard As Rock (Part 3)

Printed in Great Britain
by Amazon

54646539R00153